Light Transports

Commutes

Editor: Steve Dearden

route

First Published by Route
PO Box 167, Pontefract, WF8 4WW
e-mail: info@route-online.com
web: www.route-online.com

ISBN: 1 901927 30 X

Editor:
Steve Dearden

Thanks to:
Emma Smith, Isabel Galan, Ian Daley
GNER, Network Rail, Midland Mainline
and First TransPennine Express

Cover Design:
Steve Dearden and Andy Campbell

Printed by Bookmarque, Croydon

A catalogue for this book is
available from the British Library

Route is an imprint of ID Publishing
www.id-publishing.com

This book was possible thanks to support from
Illuminate. Illuminate is supported by the Millennium
Commission, Arts Council England, The National Lottery,
Yorkshire Culture, Yorkshire Forward, Bradford Metropolitan
District Council

Stories

Introduction

Welcome to Light Transports, reads to get you from A to B via somewhere else, each lasting a commute.

Four stories exploring how we move through the world. Alecia McKenzie is a Commonwealth Prize winning writer from Jamaica published by Peepal Tree Press in Leeds, her African heroine surfaces as an illegal domestic in Belgium. The Malawian poet Jack Mapanje lives in York where he is reclaiming the time he lost in the political prisons of Hastings Banda by writing his prison diary, from which we have some of the first published extracts. The characters in the stories by MY Alam and Sumeia Ali operate in the cities of northern England, caught between the exaggerated world of gangster bling and the mundane necessities of going straight – catching the train, holding down the day job. Four stories exploring how sometimes, we live between worlds.

These stories are locally grown or locally sourced – you can get in touch with the vibrant writing and reading going on in the Yorkshire region by visiting www.light-transports.net where there is much more on the writers in this book as well as links to the people who publish new writing and put on events in the region.

Steve Dearden

Gone To The Dogs (Madame)
Alecia McKenzie

She breezes in, shedding her coat and two Valentino shopping bags on an armchair. She always seems in a hurry though I never know what for. People who don't know her would easily believe she has countless important things to do, but I suppose that's the secret of success: look busy, always hurry, even if at the end of the day you can't say exactly what you've done.

Me, I have no time to try to look busy. I've heard her telling her husband that I'm too slow and that she doesn't know how long I'll last, but she has already gone through five cleaning ladies this year. And it's only May. I've been here seven weeks now and it looks like I'm going to set a record.

'Is lunch ready?' she says to me.

'Yes, I'll serve it,' I answer, going towards the kitchen.

I feel her tense, waiting for me to say 'Madame' but the day I turned thirty I decided to stop using the word. Her name is Madeleine Lasotte, and in my mind I call her la sotte, but to her face I say 'Madeleine' – it's close enough to 'Madame' I think.

She follows me to the kitchen, stopping just inside the door. She is a beautiful woman at first glance: thin, blonde and green-eyed. Yet something is not quite right about her face – it has a hard, masculine quality that jars with the perfect body. The thing that people always notice first though is her clothes. She dresses as if she has to go and pose for *Vogue*, but she is a beauty consultant after all so I guess she has to look the part. Consultant – it's a word I've learnt since I came here and it's what I would like to be some day. A domestic consultant, teaching people how to dust, how to clean a toilet bowl right.

'Have you prepared enough for two?' she asks.

'Yes.'

She waits a bit, clears her throat and goes out. Let her fire me for not saying Madame, I couldn't care less. Domestics are scarce in this city, people are always asking me if I can't spare a day for them – they have so much ironing to do, dust balls are piling up under the bed, they need someone to stay with their kids for a few hours, their husband is complaining that he can't remember the last time he had a proper meal. I've never been out of a job in all the years I've lived here. I work from Monday to Friday, nine to five. On Saturdays and Sundays I enjoy myself with Errol. Saturday nights we go to *La Genese* on Avenue de la Toison d'Or and dance to Zairian music and reggae till three in the morning. Sundays we go to a five o'clock movie. Last week we saw *Paradise*, about a man who secretly kills off his neighbours one by one because all his life he'd had to live in a tacky little room and now he wanted to have a whole street to himself for once. I liked it, although I didn't see why they had to show all the killings in detail.

Imagine wanting a street to yourself, though. I don't

mind my one room at the Jacques Brel youth hostel. It's cheap and people leave me alone. Before I moved there, I was a live-in for a year and it drove me crazy. No privacy, people always watching your coming and going, and feeling they can call on you to do all kinds of things during your off-hours. And sometimes Monsieur starts getting ideas, or Madame thinks that Monsieur is starting to get ideas and watches you like a cat watching a bird.

I like my life easy, no complications. This is why I'm already thinking of moving on from la sotte because she always wants to complicate things. Take the dog, for instance. When she interviewed me for the job, she didn't tell me about the animal, who looks like a big rat but who she swears is a dog. He needs to be walked twice a day, first thing when I arrive and last thing before I leave. I thought the whole reason for walking him was to let him do his business outside, on the sidewalk or in the park up the road. But no, Mister Dog is a nervous animal and often has accidents in the house. And who is supposed to clean it up? Right. La sotte would not be getting her hands dirty. I wonder what she does during the weekends when I'm not here? Monsieur probably does the honours.

But cleaning up after the dog is not the worst thing. Every time I'm out walking him people think I'm in the mood for a chat. Nothing starts conversation in this city more than having a dog trotting along beside you. 'Quel joli chien,' they say. *What's his name? How old is he? Quel race est-il?*

They always want to know that: what 'race' Mister Dog is. Usually I say: 'I think he's North African, but

11

he's afraid of discrimination so please don't tell anybody.' They leave us alone after that. When I used to babysit and I took the children out for a walk, no one even glanced at them. And when I'm out alone, most people avoid my eyes – even people who are in the same boat as myself. But Mister Dog gets loving glances and questions about his race.

La sotte said the dog was a present from Monsieur, who must have chosen an animal that would remind her of him. Monsieur is a short, thickset man with a square face and eyes that seem always to be searching for something. He owns an investment company and has had a few run-ins with the tax people, I've heard, but then that's all anyone I've ever worked for seems to talk about – taxes and the rotten government.

Monsieur makes me uneasy, especially because of the way he carries on with his wife. He is always brushing back her blond hair with his hand, removing invisible pieces of fluff from her clothes or caressing her bottom as she passes him. Yet when his eyes meet mine, I can see that he doesn't love her. When I arrive most days, he's just leaving for work and he always gives her reminders: 'Don't forget to go to the hairdresser today', or 'Don't forget to get your nails done'. And this is to a woman who always looks perfect. The first time he did it, I thought they were going out that evening, but soon I recognised the mockery in his voice. I pretend to be deaf most mornings. I just put the leash on Mister Dog, take him out and by the time I come back, she has gone as well, to visit a client or to the gym, hairdresser or stores. She always comes back by noon.

Their house is on Avenue Louise. It's really an apartment but it's bigger than any house that I've ever been in. It fills one whole floor of a huge building and the corridors seem to stretch for miles. The walls are covered with paintings – only paintings, no photographs – and the furniture is dark, shiny mahogany. The armchairs are the kind that old people like, high and hard, so that when they sit down it's not too difficult to get up. The chairs are placed in such a way that three people cannot sit comfortably to have a conversation, for each person would find himself looking at a painting. No cosy circles here. Once you've visited the house, it's easy to realise that she used to work in a gallery before she moved on to beauty.

I hear the front door slam as I finish putting the food on the table. Monsieur is home too for lunch. As they sit down to eat, I go to the kitchen to eat my sandwich and drink from my bottle of Spa. He rarely talks at lunchtime and she never stops. I often wonder how some people who never seem to do anything can be an authority on so many things. She is talking today about the rich carpet manufacturer who has been arrested for evading millions of francs in taxes.

'This country, Jean-Claude, it's going to the dogs,' she says. 'Why do they have to arrest a man who provides employment to so many people? Doesn't he contribute enough to the economy?' Jean-Claude doesn't reply, and she continues with her ranting.

My lunch finished, I start cleaning the first of the four bathrooms. When I told Errol they had four bathrooms, he said, 'Boy, they must be full of shit.'

Errol and I have been friends for about a year and a half and he keeps me laughing. He is from Jamaica and we met at the Cartagena club, where he was playing the drums in a salsa band. Salsa was a big thing here then; some people spent every Saturday night salsaing away. I never tried to do it because I feel that if you're not born in a certain country, you shouldn't try to do its dance. But I like to listen to the music. I was at the Cartagena with Dolores, a cleaning lady from the Dominican Republic who loves to dance; when she hits the floor, everyone else looks like a robot. At one point during that night she dragged me out on the dance floor to teach me her moves, but I just danced in my own way, letting the beat move my hips. Afterwards at the bar, Errol came over, introduced himself, and offered to buy us a drink. At first I thought he was interested in Dolores, but he asked for my phone number. We went to our first movie the next day.

I've finished with the fourth bathroom and am getting started on the first of the five bedrooms when la sotte comes in and sits on the bed.

'Tshana,' she says. 'Ah, I don't know how to tell you this.'

'Yes?'

'Well, somebody came by this morning asking for you while you were walking Misha.'

My hand with the duster goes still.

'Yes?'

'It was a policeman.'

'What did he want?' I ask, my voice hoarse.

She hesitates, studying her reflection and mine in

the mirror of the dressing table. I look at myself too: I am all right, despite the silly little apron. When I was a teenager in Ghalia, I never had to worry about admirers – people used to tell me that my face, if not my body, looked like Iman's before she had that car accident. And even now, over here, men still look at me in the street. La sotte and I are around the same height though I'm not as thin; my eyes are brown, and my skin is a lot darker than hers despite her many hours at the sunbank.

'You know, Tshana, when I interviewed you for this job, I didn't ask you to show me your papers because I needed someone to work so badly.'

I keep silent.

'The policeman who came this morning says you might be here illegally – you know they are cracking down on everybody. But is it true? You told me you'd been in this country for eleven years.'

I smile. 'I have been here for eleven years.'

'So how can you be illegal?'

'It doesn't really matter,' I answer. 'Do you want me to leave?'

'No, no.' She waves her hand impatiently, a flash of red nails. 'You work well, even if you are a bit slow. And your cooking is fantastic. Have you noticed that Jean-Claude is coming home more often for lunch now? If there is one problem it's that you are not very nice to Misha. You could talk to him and stroke him a bit – he's a dog who needs a lot of affection. Apart from that, I'm quite satisfied. But I don't want policemen coming to my house.'

'I can leave,' I say again.

'Are you listening? There must be some way we can fix this. Everything is fixable, you know. Have you ever tried to get your papers? How did you come here in the first place? Tell me about it.' She pats the bed beside her while I stare at the spot without moving. I wish she would leave me to get on with the work, or fire me. I don't like this sudden cosiness.

'There isn't much to tell,' I say. 'I came here with the ambassador from my country and his family. I was their housekeeper. They were recalled, and I stayed.'

'And how did you manage?' Her steady, clear gaze makes me uncomfortable. 'You must have been only nineteen when you came. How old were you when they left?'

'Nineteen going on twenty. It was no problem. You can always get cleaning or cooking jobs, no matter where you are,' I say.

'And nobody guessed?'

'That I didn't have papers? Few people care about that as long as you remove their dust.'

'Mmmm,' she says. 'You're very smart.'

She gets up and comes over to stand in front of me, the loud metallic Pierre Buglier perfume choking my nostrils. She looks up into my eyes, and I step back, uneasy.

She gives one of her rare smiles. 'Never mind,' she says, and starts walking out of the room.

'But what if the policeman comes back?'

'Don't worry. I'll talk to Jean-Claude about it. He may be able to do something. I have to go to the hairdresser now. Remember to walk Misha again before you leave.'

She sweeps out.

Dust, dust everywhere. Every day the same ritual, and the dust always wins. I flick the duster across the dresser and almost overturn one of her twenty bottles of perfume and lotions. I hate to be in a situation where people think they have to take care of me. I don't trust help. When people say, 'maybe we can help you' there are a million and one things behind it. Usually it makes them feel superior. Or they expect things in return. It was help that landed me in this country in the first place and now I don't know when I'll ever get back home with all the things going on there, all the killings, all the thieving.

I stop dusting for a minute and stretch my arms, stifling a scream that sometimes rises when I least expect it. I go to my bag and take out a CD. I put it in the player, turn the sound up loud and continue my work to the voice and beat of Angelique Kidjo. It always helps.

My uncle, the family's rich man. Mr Fix-it. The one with all the contacts, all the answers. How he adores the role. He owns five restaurants in Ghalia and nearly everybody who works there comes from the family. He treats them worse than the filth of Djabadan. I didn't want to be part of it when I finished high school; I had passed six 'O' levels and wanted to go to university or just to a little college somewhere but my uncle stepped in, told my father that I should train to be a cook. There's always money in cooking, he said, and my training would be free since I could do it at one of his restaurants. My father jumped at the idea because that meant somebody to help with the eleven coming up behind me. When I didn't show the right amount of gratitude for my uncle's kindness, my father hit me in the face, as if I was the one who'd told him to marry three wives he couldn't afford. I went to work for my uncle after the blue-black mark faded.

If you're smart in life, you learn to do quite well even the things you hate. I fooled them all at the restaurant. I put every ounce of anger into beating butter, sugar, eggs and flour together and still produced cakes that people couldn't get enough of. When I cut meat, I imagined I was killing the animal, but I made sure no one ever tasted the rage. I swallowed everything my uncle had to teach me and told no one about the hardening, painful lump it made in my stomach.

After seven months, I was in charge of the kitchen while Uncle Festus went off to see about opening another restaurant. I gave people their fufu, their beef stew, their yams – all with my own spice and they came back for more, bringing their friends with them. One of the regular customers at the restaurant was a man who worked at the foreign ministry. I knew he was an important man by the way my uncle fussed around him, and when Uncle Festus was away, I was expected to do the same thing. As soon as Mr Joseph Ekbangwa entered, one of the girls ran to tell me and I went out personally to ask him what he wanted. He was a tall, wide-shouldered man whose fleshy face was always serious. The bulging eyes told you not even to think about getting familiar, and he made sure his aura of power stretched for yards.

As I took his order, he would look me slowly up and down, making me feel as if someone were leisurely painting me with mud. He never paid for his meals, perhaps because he made sure my uncle didn't have to give away too much in taxes.

I'd been at the restaurant for less than a year when news came that Mr Ekbangwa was being sent to Europe as ambassador, and Uncle Festus immediately got busy organising a huge farewell bash. I didn't know then that I was supposed to be part of the goodbye present. It was only on the night of the party, when things were winding down, that Uncle Festus called me into his office to reveal my future.

'How d'you feel about going on a big aeroplane and living in a country where you can get rich in no time?' he asked me.

I frowned. Had he finally got a visa to go to America? Was he going to take me there to work in another restaurant?

'I don't know what you mean, Uncle.'

'How d'you feel about going to Belgium – a most beautiful and wealthy country?'

'Belgium? Where is that?'

'Next to France. Don't tell anybody that you went to high school and passed 'O' level, eh, because they won't believe you,' he said, cackling dryly for a minute.

'Why would I want to go to France?' I asked, holding my breath. Had he somehow managed to get me a scholarship to some French university? Sometimes foreign governments gave scholarships and it was all a matter of who you knew for you to get one. The Ekbangwas had two sons studying in New York.

19

'Not France, not France,' he said impatiently. '*Near* to France. Belgium. Mr Ekbangwa is going there and you are going with him as his housekeeper.'

I stared at Uncle Festus, not thinking of anything to say.

'I don't…'

'It's all arranged,' Uncle Festus said. 'You leave in five days.'

It was a clear, warm, sunny day when we landed in Brussels.

'I thought they said this was a rainy place,' Mrs Ekbangwa laughed to her husband. 'This feels just like Ghalia.'

Two Mercedes limousines, with white drivers, were waiting for us outside the airport and we headed smoothly away onto straight, wide, clean streets filled with shiny cars of every make. Nobody was walking or selling things on the broad grassy sidewalks; there were only buildings, sharp-edged and gleaming, their windows shooting back arrows of sunlight. When we stopped at a red light, no little boys ran out to clean the windshield. No one approached to ask if we wanted to buy drinks. Where were all the people?

As we passed what looked like residential areas, with brick houses built joined to one another, we saw a few people walking on the sidewalks; I felt a little bit more at ease, but my excitement at being in a new place didn't smother my discomfort.

The cars finally took us to a huge house set far back from the road in a neighbourhood that shrieked money. I waited until Mr Ekbangwa and his wife had got out of their car before I stepped out of the one behind.

'Welcome to Tervuren,' the driver said. I felt a rush of pride. What a nice embassy we had in this country.

A portly woman dressed in a grey skirt suit and red silk blouse was waiting in front of the door to greet us. 'Welcome to your new home, Mr Ambassador and Mrs Ekbangwa. I hope you like it. When you've rested I'll take you to the embassy.' It hit me then that this was the house; I would have to clean this big hell of a place by myself.

The woman led us inside and began showing us around, her voice getting nervous as both the Ekbangwas became more and more tight-lipped. When we had seen the seven bedrooms, the spacious office, the maid's studio, the three bathrooms and four separate toilets, Mr Ekbangwa said, 'This is it? You couldn't find anything better?'

The woman seemed close to tears as she explained, 'We looked at about fifty houses, Mr Ambassador. Most of them had only two bathrooms and toilets. This is the best we could find.'

Mr Ekbangwa made an ugly grunting sound in his throat. He looked outside at the stretch of land around the house then announced to the air that he was going to rest and would visit the embassy tomorrow. He headed towards the biggest bedroom while Mrs Ekbangwa asked the woman from the embassy if they had received her grocery list and whether there was any food in the house.

'We stocked the fridge and the cupboards. Everything you wanted is there, except for the fish.

That will be delivered tomorrow.'

'Tshana, cook us some lunch,' Mrs Ekbangwa told me.

The rain started that evening, a persistent drizzle that went on for days, and the sunshine that had greeted us was replaced by a cold greyness. Even my bones felt chilled, and though I'd never longed for sunshine before, I began to do so now. I even missed my father, his bickering women and my greedy half-brothers and sisters.

Still, it didn't take long for me to get into the rhythm of cleaning the big house; after three or four weeks things became relatively routine. You do the kitchen and all the bathrooms first, and then work your way from room to room. And you prepare lunch for Mrs Ekbangwa; and dinner for her, the ambassador and their guests if they have any.

During my free hours, I walked around Tervuren, staring at the big houses and wondering what people had to do to own one. The third week I discovered the museum, set in a humongous park where the neatly mowed grass seemed to stretch for miles. Tervuren's Royal Museum for Central Africa was filled with masks, traditional furniture, spears, drums, and stuffed lions, leopards, hyenas and all kinds of birds. There was even an elephant, whose glassy eyes were the only part of him that didn't look alive. I went from object to object, in admiration and respect – if you had to loot, this was the way to do it. When I left the building, I breathed deeply; it was a relief to walk again in the park where the vast space seemed to be waiting for something – a pageant or a parade.

I began spending most of my spare time in the park or wandering around the village, and after a few weeks I found the cemetery, a cemetery with the graves of Africans who'd died a hundred years before. I asked an old man who worked at the village church about the graves and he told me the story. In 1887, he said, Belgium hosted a World Expo, and 267 people from Congo were invited to come during the months of July and August to be real-life exhibits in a make-believe Congolese village in Tervuren. But that summer was a bad one and several of the Africans got ill and had to spend time in a hospital especially made for them. Seven died, but the rest survived and went back home.

'They were very happy to come here,' the old man said. 'They had a good time, and they got many presents when they left.'

I smiled and thanked him for his story. 'You have a good day,' I said.

After spending time in the park, I hurried back home in the afternoon to prepare dinner, and I always made sure to get there on time. Mrs Ekbangwa was easy enough to live with as long as you obeyed her rules and responded immediately to her barked orders. She never said 'please' or 'thank you' but overall she was quite harmless. Him, though, I couldn't stand. His eyes, when he looked at me, made me think of a frog, and I kept waiting for his leap. In preparation, I pushed my chest of drawers up against the bedroom door each night.

Before he could make his move though, he got notice saying he was recalled. Coup and different government – five months after we had left Ghalia. Mrs Ekbangwa allowed me to phone home when we heard the news, but my mother – wife Number Two, the calm one – laughed at my worries about the family. Life goes on, she said. Uncle Festus is a friend of the general. But stay where you are if you can, there's nothing for you to come back to.

I helped the Ekbangwas to pack, closing my ears to their fury when they found out I had no intention of leaving this 'most beautiful and wealthy country' to go back home.

'Well, we'll keep your passport,' the ex-ambassador said. 'Let's see what you're going to do without it.'

I didn't reply, just kept on putting things in boxes.

The night before they were to leave, the frog attempted to leap, but found the way barred. He would have had to push over the chest of drawers and wake Mrs Ekbangwa to succeed. He croaked obscenities through the keyhole until I stuffed a piece of toilet paper into it. The next morning, I didn't wait to say goodbye. I got up at six, took a bus and tram to Rue Traversière and checked into a youth hostel. You can live a cheap, peaceful life by rotating youth hostels. Six months here, six months there. A year or so as a live-in help. And then back to start the cycle again. You meet people from all over the world in youth hostels; it's a way of travelling without a passport.

As for work, as I like to say, everybody needs their dust removed.

Angelique Kidjo sings in a language I don't understand except for one song: 'Agolo'. 'Please don't forget Ife, where we all come from,' she sings. And I think back to what I learned in primary school, about King Oduduwa, and his sons and grandsons going out from the city of Ife to build kingdoms everywhere. I sing along to Angelique's chorus – and feel my spirits lift. And I laugh when I realise that I'm actually living in a kingdom here.

When the CD ends, I take Mister Dog for his walk, going over to the Ponds of Ixelles. I like this part of Brussels, with the tall townhouses and the flowers coming out now around the water. Mister Dog always barks at the swans, ducks and other birds in the ponds, while they just ignore him. I like birds, but I'm trying hard to feel affection for Mister Dog as well. I try out a new phrase on him: nice doggy. It makes me feel like an idiot, but I say it again: nice little doggy. Then I stroke him, and he responds by licking my hand. La sotte is right; he's a dog who needs affection.

Over the next few weeks, I make sure she sees that Mister Dog and I can have long conversations. I talk to him non-stop when she's around, and he looks up at me with big, watery eyes. When I tell Errol about it, he howls and says, 'Tshana, you going to the dogs, man.' His laughter stabs me, but I don't let him see it. He has no papers either and although he likes to talk about us renting an apartment and living together, we can't do that without a residence card. I don't really know if I want to set up house with Errol, but I'm getting tired of being a non-person, of walking in fear of the police. An ID card here says you're part of the human race, and Errol should know that more than anyone else.

One early morning last year, after he had finished playing at the club, the police stopped him as he walked back to the room that his employer rented for him. The police asked for his ID card and Errol told them he'd only been visiting the country for three months and didn't have his passport with him. Before the lie was finished, he found himself in their car, speeding off to the police station. There, two of the policemen treated his face as if it were a punching bag. They laughed as they hit him, calling him names he'd never heard before in French. They released him the next day, after the club-owner – a woman with friends in the right places – came to see them with her lawyer. Since then he has been left alone, but something similar could happen to him again, or to me.

So I talk to Mister Dog, and la sotte is talking to a lawyer about getting me my papers. She has said it won't be easy because I've been here too long and I don't fit the right categories: no political group wants to kill me and I don't come from an 'ethnic minority' whose land is being seized. But she still believes that something can be done and she has made me take passport pictures and fill out all kinds of forms.

I think about this when I take Mister Dog for his walk. I've even started telling him stories as we get friendlier. Once upon a time, I recite for him, there was a beautiful woman named Memai who was the pride of her homeland. For miles around, people swapped tales of her loveliness and every man of marrying age dreamt of becoming her husband. But her father, a chief, guarded her well because he felt she was fit for a king. He hoped that someone strong and rich would come along to marry Memai, and at the same time help the chief to fight his enemies, for things weren't going well in the land where Memai lived. Her people walked in fear of being captured by the ruler of a nearby kingdom. Every few days he sent his warriors to Memai's homeland where they would seize young men and women and take them away to be slaves. Memai's people tried to fight back but they were unsuited to war, having been farmers and craftsmen for decades.

The chief didn't know what to do. He sent the word out that whoever could vanquish the evil king's warriors would win Memai's hand and become chief of her homeland. But before anyone could come forward, there was another raid and Memai herself was captured by the king. When he saw her beauty, he immediately fell in love and couldn't bear to think of her being a slave, so he made her his fifth wife. Memai pretended to be in love with the king as well, and she tried to please him in every little thing, so much so that she became his favourite woman, the one always at his side. But even while he swore his eternal love, the king continued waging war on her compatriots, capturing them and selling them as slaves. Seeing her people torn from their homeland and sent away with foreigners started a fire of rage in Memai's chest and she knew she had to do something. One morning she set out early before anyone was awake and went to gather certain herbs that could be picked only before sunlight. Later that day she boiled the herbs and mixed them into the king's favourite meal, which he slurped up like a, well like you, Mister Dog. By sundown, the king was dead. And so Memai managed to free herself and her people, and when she went back to her homeland, they made her a priestess and she lived happily ever after.

Don't you think that would make a nice movie? I ask Mister Dog, but he looks sick. He begins making a coughing sound as if he's trying to vomit but can't. Finally something comes out, something that looks like cotton. Dogs will eat anything. He seems so unwell, though, that I decide to take him back home, and I lift him up and carry him in the crook of my arm, hoping that I won't run into Dolores or anybody else I know.

La sotte is at the apartment when I get back and she is touched to see me carrying Mister Dog. She fusses around him when I tell her what has happened, but she finally decides that he's not sick enough to take to a vet. She herself doesn't look too well. Her face seems old and worn without the make-up and she is acting nervous, distracted. Monsieur has been away on business for the past two days, so perhaps she's missing him.

I iron some shirts, dust the place and clean the bathrooms before preparing *chicon au gratin* for lunch. It's her favourite dish, she says but she apologises for not being able to eat as much as she would like.

When I finish working in the afternoon, she calls me into the living room and asks me to sit down. She stares at me intently when we're facing each other, and I think: here we go again. Have the police been back?

'Tshana, I have to ask you a favour,' she begins.

'Yes. What is it?'

'I have to go away for a week or so. I must leave this evening and I don't really know when I'll be back. So I want you to take Misha home with you. Could you do that?'

I look at Mister Dog, who has come to lie next to my feet, and I purse my lips. This is a bit much, isn't it? But I don't suppose anyone will care at the youth hostel.

'Okay,' I tell her. 'No problem.'

'Je vous remercie,' she says. 'And while I'm away, don't bother to come to clean the apartment. I'll call you when I get back.' She picks up Mister Dog, kisses him (I turn my head away) and gives him to me.

I feel self-conscious on the tram as I travel with Mister Dog, but to my amazement, people smile at me in a friendly, indulgent fashion. And the woman I end up sitting beside makes the inevitable comment: *Quel joli chien, quel race est-il?*

The receptionist at the youth hostel makes no comment when I enter, only slightly raises an eyebrow when he says 'Bonsoir, ça va?' But in the evening there's trouble – from Errol.

'You should've told her "no",' he says. 'I don't want to have to look at this dog every time I come here. In fact, I might just stop coming until you give it back.' But I know the problem is not the dog. Something else is bothering Errol, something that he manages to confess deep into the night when Mister Dog is out of sight under the bed. He's tired of being stuck in one place, he says. He wants the freedom to travel, to be able to wave his passport under any immigration official's nose, and someone has offered him the chance of attaining that freedom.

'Who?'

'Marguerite, she wants to marry me.'

I burst out laughing, and Mister Dog gives a frightened bark from under the bed. Marguerite Cloquet is the owner of the club where Errol plays. She is an attractive woman, short and thin with long reddish hair and blue eyes. She isn't a day younger than fifty but dresses as if she's seventeen.

'The police was hassling me again the other night, you know Tshana. I can't stand it any more. So that's why Marguerite suggested this. It would just be a business thing. You and I could still go out together…'

I'm still laughing when he leaves.

I spend the next day in bed, getting up only to feed Mister Dog and to take him outside when he seems too nervous.

The second day, I take him for a long walk around the Parc de Bruxelles to prevent us both going mad in the little room. It's a rare sunny day but I still feel numb and cold, although Mister Dog makes me smile when he chases the pigeons.

On the third day after Errol's announcement, I wake up with a plan: I will go to the Ghalia embassy and ask them to send me back home, and I'll have to take Mister Dog to a shelter and send a letter to la sotte telling her where she can find him. But as I get ready to leave my room, the receptionist comes to tell me that the postman has a package for me and that I have to sign for it.

It's a big package, and I take it to the room and open it with trembling fingers, while Mister Dog looks on. It has to be something from Errol, I think. The box contains a red felt hat and a matching short-sleeved red dress with buttons down the front, both bearing the Valentino label. Under the dress there is a thick brown envelope. I open it and pull out a passport which has my name and my picture in it. Between the middle pages of the passport there are five 10,000-franc bills, and I count them several times, clumsily. There is also an ID card sealed in plastic, and a folded piece of white paper, which I quickly open.

Dear Tshana,

I guess you've heard the news by now so you know to keep away from the apartment. Anyway, these are for you. The money is to help you take care of my little darling Misha. Please don't give him away.

Madeleine Lasotte

I don't know what the letter means, but I plan to find out. First though, I put on the dress and hat and admire myself in the mirror. I've never looked this good before. I wish Errol could see me right now. I pick up Mister Dog and walk through the lobby of the youth hostel as if I own the place. We stroll down to the nearby newspaper shop and I buy two copies of *Le Soir*, one from today and one from yesterday. The man behind the counter falls over himself calling me 'Madame' and asking if there's anything else I want. What a difference a few pieces of clothes can make.

On the sidewalk, I scan the pages quickly and there in black and white is Monsieur alongside a story about his running off with his clients' money. In the past two days, police have been searching his office and his home, says the article, but have found no trace of him or his wife. It is not clear whether they have absconded together or whether she went into hiding after he left. The police are now questioning people who worked for the couple.

I don't wait to read the rest of the story but rush back to the youth hostel and throw my few belongings into a suitcase. I touch the passport and ID card lovingly before putting them in my handbag. Then I pick up Mister Dog, hurry up the road to Place Madou and take a taxi to the train station.

Mister Dog sits on my lap as the train starts moving. I stroke his brown-black hair. 'How does Amsterdam sound, eh Misha? And after that Paris? You know they love doggies there.' I smile to myself, a smile that scares me when I see it reflected in the train window. No, Errol, I haven't gone to the dogs. You have. Me, I'm getting the hell out of here.

Junk Food

M Y Alam

The old faces throw a party in my honour. They're all there, except for Smoke, who's sent a deputy instead, telling me the man's out of town. Even Smoke's little messenger knows this is a line but no one wants to spoil the buzz. Slapping my back, one by one they tell me well done for keeping quiet and being stand up. I smile and laugh through, wanting to be elsewhere, only sticking around because it makes them feel better, somehow relieved. My friends, they're older but don't seem to be much wiser. Showing a few more lines, bellies hanging lower but no change inside the head, where it counts. Losers then and losers now; once the meet and greet's over, they start bitching about everything except themselves. *Nothing new, even less to do; scan the paper, down a brew.* A four-by-six pad wasn't all that bad by comparison. My own space, a regular supply of reading material and time to think. Might have been shut away for a few years, but I wasn't dying on my feet like I am here.

With party time over and the cost of living to be met, I start seeking a job. Two weeks later, the son of a bitch is still hiding. I hit former employers, call on shops, warehouses and factories. No dice, giving me the same *don't call us we'll call you* shit. Seems no one's looking to hire a man with my kind of CV. I still got options, the Job Centre tell me. I put my name down with the big fast food joints but the false apologies and synthetic expressions say it all: from up on high me and my kind are memo-d out of the McEmployment loop. I try everywhere but it's not happening: can't even get an interview stacking shelves in some shitty Scandinavian supermarket chain. If I could get my foot in the door, I'd convince them I'm safe, reliable, honest and value for money but one tick in the wrong box is all it takes.

I invest in case I get lucky: Scooby Doos, white shirt, inoffensive tie and dull as dishwater grey two-piece sewn by *John R. Slater Bespoke Tailor* according to the label. Bought from a charity shop, the outfit leaves me a tenner poorer but the hardship might pay off. The old maid behind the counter nods reassuringly and tells her colleague:

'It could have been made for him.'

'Made for him, yes,' says the other old love.

I rehearse my interview technique over and over, sometimes in full costume, in front of the wardrobe mirror, sometimes while lying awake in bed at night. *Well, I've had time to reflect and I think I've matured. In some ways it was the best thing that could have happened. Straightened me out in no time. I'm a better person, now. Yes, you could say that: I was mixing with some very bad company. Looking on the bright side, it got me away from them. I know, it's a price to pay but it was worth it. Definitely, I do genuinely think I've learnt a lot and I'm just happy to be given a chance.* The script is a variation of the bullshit the probation service got to hear, but this feels different because after a while, I'm starting to believe it.

The days roll into weeks and I start doing something that I'd always thought beyond me: worrying. Being straight and being skint is not sustainable. I can't survive on the handout the government gives me, no one can. Like the old ladies in the charity shop, I get by, skimping on costs where and when I can: foot patrol, Adam's Ale, cut-price food and duty free tobacco. I stay occupied to kill the time: clean the flat, read a book, watch some telly, develop my hook.

*

The landlord's the only company I get. Every other night he comes for a quick inspection; checks to make sure his place is still his place. I get the impression that he's half expecting to turn up and find the flat converted into a crack factory, a whorehouse or some such den of iniquity. It's not exactly a palace: furniture's fucked, carpets are crappy and the wash basin's buggered. It's a shit hole but it's the best I can do and for now, it's home.

Nearly two months after the party, Smoke's at my door. I hadn't forgotten, just didn't want to think about the problems he'd bring. Four years since we last met, give or take. Used to believe ours was an honest connection. The student learnt a few tricks while the master exploited his trainee's talent as a salesman of all goods illicit. I made a lot of money; Smoke made more. I lost every penny and did a few courses in Crook College. Smoke stayed free, solvent and protected.

'How's things?' I ask.

Smoke doesn't just move drugs. Turns out he'll sell anything, even his dealers, especially if his own freedom is at stake.

'Everything good?' I add.

I grew to hate the man. It became a part of me, an extra layer of fat under my skin, a disease in my blood, a growth in my head.

'All good,' he says.

No surprise to hear him still talking in reverse. Bad means good, pain means gain and honour means less than a half-promise from a politician on the way out.

'Yeah, good and that. No worries.'

Smoke's riding with Young Blood. A rising star, no older than a school kid, he saunters in like he's already arrived. Full of himself, same as me after I fell for Smoke's bullshit. Disappointing but Smoke's M.O.'s not surprising: get them young, impressionable and, according to armies of coppers, social workers and community leaders, in need of *successful male role models who they can identify with*. Find them, win their confidence and gain their respect by giving them sex, violence and money: shag a slag, abuse a user, flash the cash. Then step back and set them free to earn. It's not a bad living, catching a few crusts from Smoke's table, especially when he's reminding you *there's more where that came from*.

'You not busy?' asks Smoke.

'No, not really.'

Young Blood intrigues me. The kid's got the look that took me the best part of two years to perfect. Lean, tough looking, flexing his arms and chest better than a steroid chugging bodybuilder.

'Just warming down, like,' he says, reacting to my interest. 'Had a workout with the weights. Suppose you know about that, like. Weights, keeping trim.'

'You need to look after yourself.'

He steps toward me, hand outstretched, smiling his tits off. We shake, and he starts laying out a load of chatter, calling me *Bro* like he calls everyone, including his old man, *Bro*. Telling me shit I don't want or need to know. I've heard it all from others just like this one. Stepping up like we're tight or could be; talking to me like they know me when they don't even know my name. To know a man, you got to know what he's done, where he's been and which side of the compass leads him home. Hell, I don't know most of that myself. Up and comers, they got this need to sell themselves even though a man's not looking to buy.

He continues laying the gloss better than a used car salesman. I've seen speed freaks get this way but this boy's high on life and won't come down until Smoke drops him. Always *getting* something: laid, wasted, away with it. He might be one of those crazies who jabbers even though no one's listening – missed his medication, maybe. Now *keeping it* something: *real, street, ghetto*. Precisely what ghetto we talking about, my man? No ghettos in this town that I know – just places where people live and places where they don't. Even if there was a ghetto, there'd be nothing good about it. Paradise for thieves, burglars, jackers, muggers, dealers and their junkies but for everyone else, violence, filth, misery and pain. Idiots glamorise it; write stupid, immature and blindingly bad poetry about it but they're fools, misguided or just plain deluded. Better

39

off sweeping streets, stacking shelves and weaving baskets.

Smoke, smiling his metal-toothed mouth my way, listens to his young apprentice like a teacher, if not proud of the performance, then chuffed to bits with the kid's stamina. I wish I felt the same. Sounds rehearsed, like Young Blood's been perfecting the script for weeks, months even. I wonder where he gets them from, these little phrases that trickle off his tongue better than the curses he's been spitting since he was old enough to mimic all those dead and dying rappers he hears. *Old school...hood...homeboys.* Words without anything real or honest behind them. Fantasy. A teenager's wet dream. Old school? How *old school* can a sixteen year old who lives with his folks – semi detached, garage by the side, Volvo in the drive and IKEA on the floor – ever be? *Hood?* Since when is surburbia anything but the hood? *Homeboys?* Won't see them for dust once his old man ships him over to Pakistan and taxes his passport. Some poor waif, deserving a hell of a lot more, will get tethered to this idiot for the rest of her life. And why? Because Young Blood here actually believes all the smoke that's being blown up his arse.

'Making it happen and that,' he says. 'Big time. Bitches, dollars – dollar-dollar-bling...game like a natural.'

I bet his mother's real proud, too.

'That's really something.'

Smoke passes him a half joint to suck on; a pacifier, least for now.

'Wondering,' says Smoke. 'About stuff.'

'Stuff?'

'You know,' he sniffs, and then, sounding like one of those counsellors. 'You and me. Stuff we need to resolve.'

'Thought it was resolved.'

'That's what you're saying?'

'I done what I had to do. We got nothing else to talk about.'

'Had no choice,' he says, eyeballing me, puffing his chest out and then stepping up close; his posture not matching his words. 'Filth set me up with a stack of gear. Brief saying twelve to fifteen. Couldn't do that – not me.'

'I understand.'

'Owe you,' he nods. 'Wanna make it up to you. Put all that behind us. Offer for you. Me and you at the top: fifty-fifty.'

I try to sound sincere but it's hard. This is idiotic, this offer. Lame.

'I can't see it. Done a lot of thinking inside. A lot of working out, too.'

'Yeah? What you work out?'

'Just one thing: I don't want to go back. So thanks, but I'm passing.'

No matter what you say to Smoke, he'll always figure you're working him with some angle, some double meaning. This paranoia is not a flaw he was born with, he got this way after he fell for the charms of Mary Jane.

'All good,' he says. 'Glad to hear you're on the straight. Should have known. Had to ask.'

He looks around the room again and reaches into his pocket.

'Tell you what,' he says, passing me a wad of fifties, couple of grand at least, 'get yourself set up.'

I don't go for the money and tell him:

'It's not necessary. Straight means straight.'

'Kidding?' he says, laughing. 'My money no good?'

'Maybe it's me with the problem,' I say, smiling back, the hatred I'd almost conquered starting to bubble inside my gut.

All hard faced again, he gives me his upset and offended gangster routine, straight out of the text book: 'Serious? Don't want my money?'

'Thanks, but no thanks.'

'Alright,' he says. 'Your way.'

I'd be naïve to think that's it. He can't let this drop as it is. Either I'm with him or against him; there is no middle ground, no such thing as a neutral in Smoke's scheme of things. Allowing a man to go straight isn't an option. If I'm out there and no longer in his service, I'm a liability and he can't have that. Trouble is, I know his moves before he does. Despite his calm and friendly exit, I got a feeling he's already planning our next meeting, an exchange which will resolve things once and for all.

*

Feels criminal, this midnight flit out of Bradford to our richer and more upwardly mobile cousin down the road. It's trying, but no way this Smith can keep up with that firmly middle-class, economically achieving and socially climbing Jones. Like Smoke, it's all front. Bigger, stronger, better. Look closer and it's not so wonderful; there's fewer divisions in the world of boxing. Maybe it's always been about colour but the shade of your wad, not your skin, matters most.

The vibe: business, money, confidence. Everyone loves Leeds, the city mine could have been. Bigger spaces, louder sounds and brighter visions. The centre stacked with marble and layered with glass, outer edges stamped with Mock Tudor and lined with block paving; designer suits, thick-knot ties, four-wheel drives and GTIs, sculpted arses, lipo-d thighs, work-life lows and cocaine highs. *Bad arse*, but like Smoke's way of working, it's the in-between zones where another kind of story takes shape. Red brick islands sitting in oceans of cracked tarmac and breaking glass; here be monsters big and bold, dodgy goods bought and sold, kids with pitbulls and knockoff gold.

I hole up in a zone that reminds me of home. Cheap and practical, safe and familiar once you manage to tune out all the interference. Doesn't look like much. The crap on the streets and the lack of anything green are all superficial details that deter most prospective first-time buyers, renters and the fussier squatters. Not an adventure, more like a survival course, but an experience worth having. Anything that wakes you up and makes you stronger can't be all bad. If you can make it here, you can make it anywhere. New York is Disneyland by comparison.

Thinking things will be different in a city of opportunity, I try my luck again in the work market. Same old story: fill in the forms, make the calls and wait. At least I don't have to worry about Smoke; three weeks since I left and I've not heard a thing.

Functioning on autopilot, life once again becomes a blur of breathing, moving and occasional thinking. Daytime television followed by afternoon, evening and night-time television. Every day I go for a walk and wind up in the library. On the way back, I stop at a little old coffee bar that's not yet overrun with students, office types or idiots who spend all their waking moments talking with people they don't know or care to see. The old Italian woman behind the counter makes good coffee and there's always a noise playing on the jukebox that sounds like music. Back home, I clean the pad, maybe water the plants and then settle down to reading whatever the librarian tells me is good. So far, he's not been right once. If I can face it, I'll watch some junk TV but most times I stick with junk radio – some presenter talking shit about all the things he craves: crime, drugs, celebrity and alien women who cover themselves up. As evening draws in, I'll heat and eat something out of a tin and then go for another walk, wandering through the neighbourhood like a tourist. I can't say I've made any friends but I've not made any enemies yet.

I take a train back into Bradford so I can check in with a guy called Compton, a dead ringer for someone who hates being a probation officer more than he hates the wife and the in-laws put together. He seems to understand the reasons for my self-imposed exile but he's not one for cutting me slack:

'Find a job. You can't keep signing on forever.'

*

44

Mr Happy Fried Chicken and Fast Food Bar seems unsure about setting me on. It's a job I want more than I want anything else right now, but he's taking this way too seriously. A couple of minutes into the interview, if that's what it is, he tells me his name:

'Mister Sheikh,' he says. 'Call me Mister Sheikh.'

'Okay,' I say.

Sheikh clears his throat and then starts going through a load of rules like a kid reciting times tables:

'No worker turn up late. If worker turn up late, I change wage. No worker knock off early. If worker knock off early, I change wage. No worker give backchat. If worker give backchat, I change wage…'

I get the idea, but he continues with lines he's adapted from some movie he's seen one time too many. The only thing worth knowing is Sheikh's got more greed and cunning than Wall Street and the Stock Exchange put together. Taking an unauthorised break, loud talking, clowning around…I'm surprised he doesn't get all worked up about workers farting on duty. The man's not a moron; just another arsehole thinking he's got some pull.

He makes more noises about employing a guy with my background but considering there's no queue of takers snaking down the street, I figure I got a chance. Before he makes a formal offer, he fires more questions. The way he's going on, you'd think I was marrying his daughter.

'Work before?'

'This and that,' I say, hoping he'll let it pass.

'Two career? You lucky.'

Didn't know I could take this kind of bullshit from

this kind of idiot for this length of time. Don't know whether to feel proud about my self-control or ashamed for not dropping the son of a bitch.

'I done a few things over the years.'

'Speak on,' Sheikh says, leaning back, swivelling on his chair. 'I listen.'

High and mighty types like this smug, greasy man are always looking to be taken down a notch or ten. The bad news is, I can't afford to be the one to do it. Compton's being a real pain about not paying my way through life: *Tell me, why should my taxes keep another scrounger in comfort?* Maybe he's got a point but I don't need him hassling me any more than I need Smoke and his trainees flexing down my path.

'Well?' asks Sheikh, a little impatient, now.

'Factory work, a bit of driving, some retail.'

Perhaps, now he'll quit with these bullshit questions. I should be so damned lucky; only gone and made him more inquisitive.

'Factory?'

'Production line.'

'What making?'

'Not making. Slaughterhouse: killing,' I say, noticing him flinch.

'Driving?' he asks, after clearing his throat.

'Delivery.'

'Meat?'

'Carcasses.'

'And retail?'

'Butchers.'

'Butcher, driver, killer,' he says with a sniff. 'You clean licence?'

'Still half dirty.'

'What mean half dirty?'

'Six points.'

He rocks forward, then back again and looks at me all unsure, straining like a near blind man struggling to focus.

'Okay,' he says with a builder's fake sigh, 'but understand, I talking risk with you. No second chance. One time strike and finish. Out. You understand this one?'

'I understand,' I reply. 'Thanks.'

I don't realise I'm smiling until he asks me:

'Why so funny?'

It's not funny at all. Whether it's drugs they're peddling or southern fried chicken, they're all the same. Business is business, what they sell is incidental.

'Nothing,' I say, quickly recalling a line from the spiel I memorised. 'I'm just happy to be given a chance.'

He moves forward, picks up a pen and starts doodling on a pad. This must be the bit where he tries to come across all super significant, like he matters.

'Trial period. Couple week working then review,' he says and then quickly adds: 'Okay-fair-happy-start tonight-okay?'

Two months of a quid and a half below minimum wage later, I'm still waiting for the trial period to end and for this idiot's review to begin. Can't say I've grown to appreciate the man, now that I've seen him in his environment. Matter of fact, I'm starting to develop an intense dislike for Sheikh, so much so that I fantasise about bitch-slapping him to tears. A little cruel, I know, but Sheikh's the kind of ogre even his mother couldn't love. Sitting there scratching his balls with one hand and stuffing greasy chips or nuggets of deep fried chicken into his gob with the other, I swear I've seen dogs with better manners and more likeable personalities. One sharp-minded, ignorant-aired son of a bitch with a streak of meanness a mile wide. A malicious man with a dirty mouth, more cursing than a bunch of pissed-up sailors on shore leave: *sonavabitch* this, *donkeyfucker* that. In between manning the till, feeding his already bloated face and counting his money, he barks orders worse than a prison screw looking for an easy way out of a fully fledged career crisis.

There's another three workers behind the counter. We're a team but they're the ones doing all the work, the crappiest jobs going. He doesn't know them but when I hear him go on at them, I can hear the hate. He can't bear to call them anything other than *Oi, You, Dickhead, Bastard.* Like him, they're immigrants of one description or another – the hunted, the hungry, the hopeful – legals, illegals and those who can tick every box going. Happy to be here even though they know most would rather see the back of them, or not see them at all. Hard workers: heads down, ask no questions, raise no alarm, make no trouble, cause no harm. My kind of people.

Dealing with me, Sheikh is a bit more reserved but only because he knows I've got my own map to follow. He doesn't see me as a migrant which makes me superior, the most qualified. I'm quickly promoted to second in command; a student once again, learning from another corrupt master. I take orders, use the preparation equipment, supervise the others. One of my team, a forty-something Iraqi called Ali could take a tank apart with a couple of screwdrivers and a pair of pliers, but here, he's only good for donkey work. I should count myself lucky, privileged – blessed even – because I get to use the dough machine, the mincer, the salad slicer and have access to a tacky aluminium briefcase containing a dozen blades bought from a suited and booted knocker for a fiver: look the part but they're the kind of knives that blunt after the first decent cut. I've got a soft spot for the cleaver but only because it's never been used and has that brand new sheen to its edge. Sheikh checks the case every night to make sure they're all present. Trust is not something that comes easily to him.

For those with aspirations of owning a joint like this some day, it's an apprenticeship; a place where the uninitiated in the ways of fast food on a smaller scale learn the ropes of which there are not too many: if it doesn't sleep in the oven or sit on the hot plate, it gets fried – most things can be fried; if food, utensils, equipment look clean, they're good enough to be treated as if they are clean; nothing is wasted that's why refrigerators, microwaves, sauces and garnishes were invented. If a burger does happen to catch a spot of dust, dirt or something worse, it won't matter because it contains enough antibiotics and chemicals to cure half a dozen types of VD.

The only time something close to a conversation happens with punters is when it has to: *You want*

anything on that? Mayonnaise; chilli sauce; ketchup; salad...
More fast food joints in this city than there are drug
dealers. Knowing the way the product is reared,
butchered, processed, digested then shat out before
being dredged and filtered back into the food chain, I
can't say I know which does more harm. An immoral
shotgun wedding, a forced marriage between what was
once meat, preservatives, flavourings, long-life cooking
fat and good old profit. Kebabs churned out by the
van load but not a skewer in sight. Special offers
slapped all over the walls: fried chicken with chips –
99p, cheeseburger with chips – 99p, donner kebab with
salad and sauce – 99p. Slap your coin on the counter,
mumble an order and I'm happy to oblige: *You want
anything on that? Mayonnaise; chilli sauce; ketchup; salad;
maybe half a fresh dog turd, for a change?* Could be food I
serve, a taste they savour, but it's just another poison
to swallow.

Frying, grilling and slicing for ten hours a day, six
days out of seven can be a slow death if you let it get
under your skin. You switch off and on at will; the
work can be done by a monkey, after all. Your team
keeps you going and after a while, you begin to see
each other as comrades, friends, even. During breaks
or when Sheikh's having one of his marathon half-an-
hour shits, you get to talk, listen and learn. The stories
they tell have more tragedy than anything the Greeks
could offer; the things they've seen and done make
Johnny Rambo's escapades look like gay porn flicks in
comparison. You realise you've had it easy. Like living
in a shit hole, being with this trio seems to be making
me stronger.

Fast food joints attract punks better than a ripped set of wheels gliding into *tha hood*. Being young and immature, the world lets them slide through. In the meantime the decent ones get caught up in the mix but only because they look alike: half-shaved, tram-lined, hoodie covered heads; gilded fingers, ears and necks; labelled trainers, tracksuits and tops; a bass in their voice that says more than the vocabulary they've still not managed to master.

'Donner,' the one at the front says, cocking his head like he's aping a pigeon. 'Lots of salad, lots of chilli and that, innit.'

'Anything else?'

He shakes his head at one of his punk friends and mumbles something.

'You want anything else?' I ask again.

He turns back to face me, a combination of disgust and arrogance painted vividly across his face.

'I'd tell yer if I wanted owt else. Daft bastard.'

Takes more than a copy of my younger self to work me up. It's what young punks are about. Aggressive, superior and to all intents and purposes, indestructible, if not immortal. With his homeboys getting his back, a guy flipping burgers is nothing.

'Well?' he says, leaning over the counter now, his face nearly touching mine.

I back off, and when I tell him the line I'd hear my own victims blurt, I realise I'm smiling at the memory.

'I don't want no trouble.'

One of the posse starts making his way through to

the front, all the time looking at me. Young Blood's grown broader and looks meaner since I seen him riding with Smoke. Don't know if he's got me clocked but I get out of sight and hope he hasn't made the connection. I grab Jonathan, a poet on the run from some African anti-poet dictator, and tell him:

'Take over the counter, man. I gotta take five.'

Sheikh shouts something my way but I ignore him, heading out the back to smoke something strong, drink something sweet, and think of a life long gone but, try as I might, not forgotten.

Young Blood and his posse left without much further fuss, according to Jonathan who asks me if anything's wrong a few times but then drops it when he realises this is my own problem to sort. I can't seem to get anything worked out, at least not in my head. I can't make peace with Smoke because he'll see that for what it is; weakness on my part, fear even. I can't go back with him and start selling again because I know that's the shortest cut to prison. Maybe there is another option, one that's just as painful as all the others but at least it's got a future that I can live with.

The rest of my shift is a series of fuck-ups. Fucking up the orders, fucking up the food, fucking up the delivery addresses and even fucking up team mates who keep on having to cover my failings. I can't think straight; can barely think at all and I pray for the clock to work double time. By the end, I'm ready to lay a few on the next shit-talking drunk as a way of relieving the stress. Limbs weary, feet etched with aches and a head that won't let up on throbbing. Haven't got it in me to hang around until the shutters come down and the ovens, the grills and the deep fat fryers chill out for the night. Jonathan asks me, same as he asks me every night, if I'm turning up tomorrow.

'Maybe not.'

Jonathan smiles broadly, his teeth clean, bright and perfect.

'You say that every night.'

'Could be I mean it this time.'

Sheikh, meanwhile, has been moaning about my unauthorised break, the numerous mistakes and how he's going to have to rethink my position. I've been thinking about that, too, but he needn't know the details. He docks me a fiver. I don't lose my cool. Makes no odds – he can keep his lousy job and the greasy money that he pays. I'll tell him but not tonight. He should consider himself lucky, considering the lump of poison that's banging around my head.

Sheikh calls out after me as I start to walk the few streets home, my arm weighed down and my confidence lightened thanks to a piece of metal tucked up my sleeve. I take my time, making the most of the cold, dark air that always manages to hold the nausea in check. The smell of fat stays cooked in my head, the grease clings and sticks to every part of me until I get home where I'll submerge myself in the bath for as long as the water stays warm.

As I silently tread past the ex-council properties, I hear life coming from within: lines of conversation, volleys of argument, choruses of laughter and, in one house with a broken window and pavement pizza on the doorstep, I'm sure I can hear a scream of fear, perhaps rage or possibly pleasure.

My ears prick up at the sound of a German engine drawing close behind me. I carry on walking at the same pace while the car gradually grows louder until I'm walking in its beam. I stop as the ride draws by my side. Sleek and black, sat calmly on aftermarket castors, tinted glass hiding the occupants, custom exhaust gently rasping out noxious fumes; more bling than a pimp convention. Smoke winds the glass down and hits me with the cliché I've been expecting.

'You can run,' he says, 'but you can't hide.'

The prodigy riding shotgun, itching to pop his gangster cherry, Young Blood and Smoke are a truly regular thing.

'Well?' Smoke asks, elbow propped on window opening, chin rested on hand – a gangster deep in thought. 'What can you do with an itch you can't scratch?'

I steal a look into the car and see Young Blood's not his usual chirpy self. Quiet as a mouse, one hand holding a freshly lit spliff, the other tucked into his Hilfiger jacket, holding onto something important, precious and life changing. I'm not convinced talking will do me any good. Running, like Smoke says, is only a short-term fix. Even though it's only real in Smoke's fucked up head, our problem needs to be resolved and right about now is good enough for us both, I guess. Older, bigger and stronger but not beyond me. As for Young Blood, he's just a kid who'll shit himself the minute he realises things are not going to plan. Least, I hope he will.

'Maybe it's a scratch looking for an itch that's not there,' I say.

Smoke throws his head back and starts laughing, the prelude to the action. I know his moves before he does. I just hope he's unaware of mine.

'You a poet now, Butcher?'

Sheikh's cleaver slides down the inside of my coat sleeve, the handle nestling nicely in my hand. I take a deep breath, the smell of junk food not diluted one bit.

Hold Them Tight

Jack Mapanje

Saturday, 28 November 1987.

It's about ten weeks now, I've had no news of my family and I know they have had none of me. I am getting worried, very worried. Obviously rumours of my whereabouts have been flying about, judging from the numerous stories that are reverberating within the walls of my prison. I was murdered like 'the famous gang of four' – the four senior MPs murdered in cold blood for being popular with the people – but unlike them, Life President Hastings Kamuzu Banda's hungry crocodiles in the Lower Shire Valley chewed me up alive. I was dumped at Central Prison in Zomba, Chichiri Prison in Blantyre, Maula Prison in Lilongwe, the Dzeleka Prison in Dowa district, the most notorious and isolated prison in Nsanje district – the speculations have been endless.

The truth is nobody knows where I am. University authorities never find out or even inform family of the fate of staff who are 'taken' for political reasons. The security authorities do not consider it their duty to tell the relatives of the people they abduct where they have kept them. I know this for a fact. But I find myself fretting more and more as new political prisoners are brought into cell D4. And the questions that haunt my sleepless nights are many. Has my wife lost her job? Have the children been expelled from school? Has my family been thrown out of the university house? Where exactly is my family? Are my colleagues in the department being harassed? I know I am not indispensable, but how has the redistribution of the courses I teach gone? How are my students coping?

I pluck up courage and consult TS. He suggests I have a private word with Brown who, lying on his bed, listens empathetically to my fears. And with that extraordinary generosity which fills the 'Republic of D4', as they call the cell to which I have been transferred, he fishes out two Lifebuoy Soap wrappers from his pillow of blanket-rags and a short pencil lead from his kinked hair – so kinked hair does have its use after all, I think to myself. 'Hold them tightly,' he says, pushing them into my right hand. Into my left hand he pushes his roll of toilet paper. I know his kind of game. I am about to join the famous African political prisoners who have used various wrappers or toilet paper to communicate with the outside world – Dennis Brutus, Wole Soyinka and Ngugi wa Thiong'o among them; but any feelings of getting above myself quickly evaporate as Brown announces loudly to the rest of the cellmates:

'Sorry, fellows, but our professor here wants to use the toilet.'

Ndovi and those whose beds are nearest the toilet in the corner leave the cell to give me privacy. Pingeni, reading the Bible on his bed at the other end of the cell, declares it's too hot for him to sit in the courtyard outside, he doesn't mind hearing the 'bombs' about to be blasted from the university professor's bottom! We laugh as Brown shows me how to jam a long broom handle from the kitchen against the door to keep it half-closed, a sign to those in the courtyard that someone is using the toilet, that way nobody should barge in. I begin by flushing the toilet so that Pingeni won't hear the rustle of paper as I straighten the Lifebuoy Soap wrappers, though I'm more afraid that prison guards will burst in and find me committing the unforgivable rebellion of writing to my wife. Comforted by the thought that Brown and TS will be watching out for me, I sit down on the toilet, rest my Lifebuoy Soap wrappers on the toilet roll, and begin the first of my many notes to her:

> *Dee, I am alive. Thank God. They took me to Mikuyu Prison where I am writing this. I am well. How are you, the children, Mother? Still staying in the university house? The children still at school? Not lost your job yet? I pray. No idea why I was arrested; have not been charged with any crime; the authorities hinted that someone at the university reported me directly to the Life President. If you can, find out from CC Principal K or university council chairman JT; they'll know if anybody does. Probably easiest to find out the official position from V.C. John Dubbey. Send your reply through Fr Pat but do be very careful. Tell Lan & Alice in York I am here.* Pepani *for the pain you and the children will suffer because of*

this; but miss you all very, very much. Lots of love. Daa

The second note is to Fr Pat O'Malley, a veteran of troubled times, having been in Nigeria during the Biafran civil war; he's known here as a doughty fighter for civil rights. When my university teacher Felix Mnthali, my colleague, Mupa Shumba, and other local university staff mostly from northern Malawi, were imprisoned in the 70s, it was Fr Pat who looked after some of their families. That he arrived at my house just before the police dragged me away for interrogation the day I was arrested and brought here, is typical of his generous heart.

Dear Fr Pat, Greetings from Mikuyu Prison. Thank God I survived the ordeal the day I showed you my handcuffed hands. Gave me hope to see you at the house before I was 'taken'. Maybe you've already told Landeg White at the University of York, David Munthali on sabbatical at the University of Newcastle, Neil Smith at University College London, Felix Mnthali at the University of Botswana, Hangson Msiska at the University of Stirling, Lupenga Mphande at Ohio State University, Frank Chipasula at the University of Nebraska and other colleagues, compatriots and friends all over the world about my imprisonment. Looks like someone reported me directly to H.E. without telling the police – and you know who – otherwise, I was not tried or charged with any offence. N.B. This courier has

taken incredible risks; might need some help for
transport; more of him in future, God willing, but
can be trusted completely. For all our sakes please
keep his identity and our correspondence under
wraps. I hate to think what would happen to us
all if either were discovered. Kindly pass on the
note to Mercy. Tell David Kerr about the courier
stressing the secrecy needed, hope nobody is
harassing him in the Department of Fine and
Performing Arts or you and other colleagues in our
department or the students. Send us your news, any
news, please. Love & Peace. J

Not exactly in the class of Brutus, Soyinka or Ngugi, but as I pull up my foya shorts and flush the toilet with much force and noise carefully folding my notes of Lifebuoy Soap wrappers, I feel the first shiver of pleasure and self-satisfaction since I landed in this hell-hole. I return to my bed in a self-congratulatory mood. I believe I have taken the first step to connect with the world outside, though yet again Pingeni punctures my complacency in a quiet voice without looking up from the page of the Bible he's reading.

'Doc, next time you use the toilet, flush only after the big job, the water is erratic here; you were lucky the toilet worked again after the first flush; you'd have been embarrassed.'

I accept my oversight with a grin as I move the broomstick holding the door half-closed. Brown comes in and takes back his roll of toilet paper and pencil lead. He takes my neatly folded notes and rolls them in the hem of his foya shirt, whispers that he has a partner at the Centre for Social Research in the university, who knows Fr Pat and will see he gets them. Brown simply fills me with confidence and hope; even in these conditions the respected journalist and broadcaster is informed and organised – more than enough reason to be jailed in this culture of secrecy and corruption.

That night I have the first series of disjointed dreams, and all I can recall is what's centred around my eldest uncle without whom my brother and I would not have gone to school. He had shot himself and died without proper explanation when I was a student at University College London. It later transpired that he had been frustrated by the famine of the 1980s, which Life President Banda's government claimed, typically, did not exist – no one in Banda's villages up and down the country was starving; no one had died. But in a letter to me my uncle begged to differ and wrote about how our entire extended family would starve to death if I did not intervene. Despite the pledge he had made when I was young, that he would never seek help from me when I grew up, he declared that the family was in a dire state. My student grant was too small for my family of four, but I sent him two lots of £60, the first through his son and the second through the nephew he had adopted as his son. I was to discover long after his death that he had not received the money. In fact both sons had used the money to buy food for their families instead of sending it to him to feed the larger extended family. I suspected that he had taken his life in order to show the two sons what a horrible act they had done. However, the guilt I felt for his death followed me wherever I went. I kept saying to myself that I should not have trusted my cousins with the money.

But in the dream my uncle reproaches me. 'Forget about me; you are not responsible for my death; I want you to introduce your two friends Brown and TS to Mpokonyola village to see the people there,' he says and suddenly disappears. I wake up to the prison guard's truncheon poking at my side. And as I watch the guards beat up those who want to continue sleeping, I begin to puzzle about the meaning of my dream.

Scrubbing the Furious Walls of Mikuyu

Is this where they dump those rebels,
these haggard cells stinking of bucket
shit and vomit and the acrid urine of
yesteryears? Who would have thought I
would be gazing at these dusty, cobweb
ceilings of Mikuyu Prison, scrubbing
briny walls and riddling out impetuous
scratches of another dung-beetle locked
up before me here? Violent human palms
wounded these blood-bloated mosquitoes
and bugs (to survive), leaving these vicious
red marks. Monstrous flying cockroaches
crashed here. Up there cobwebs trapped
dead bumblebees. Where did black wasps
get clay to build nests in this corner?

But here, scratches, insolent scratches!
I have marvelled at the rock paintings
of Mphunzi Hills once but these grooves
and notches on the walls of Mikuyu Prison,
how furious, what barbarous squiggles!
How long did this anger languish without
charge without trial without visit here and
what justice committed? This is the moment
we dreaded; when we'd all descend into
the pit, alone; without a wife or a child
without mother; without paper or pencil
without a story (just three Bibles for
ninety men) without charge without trial.
This is the moment I never needed to see.

Shall I scrub these brave squiggles out
of human memory then or should I perhaps
superimpose my own, less caustic; dare I
overwrite this precious scrawl? Who'd
have known I'd find another prey without
charge without trial (without bitterness)
in these otherwise blank walls of Mikuyu
Prison? No, I will throw my water and mop
elsewhere. We have liquidated too many
brave names out of the nation's memory;
I will not rub out another nor inscribe
My own, more ignoble, to consummate this
Moment of truth I have always feared!

Saturday, 19 December 1987.

I am gazing at the prison's brick wall in the courtyard, counting the holes that hide people's secret notes, broken razor blades, newspaper cuttings, needles and other items prohibited in prison, when guard commander BK shouts, 'Professor to the office!' My name ripples within the prison walls. From the prison's office block BK repeats, 'Officer in charge wants to see professor!' I put on cleaner *foya* in case my wife and children, relatives or friends have finally been allowed to visit me three months after my imprisonment. The cellmates wish me well. 'Doc, don't come back,' shouts Pingeni. 'Remember to fight for us when you're gone,' concurs Chunga. 'Just tell the world how boring and inhuman it is here,' declares Mbale. But I know this can't be my release, and before BK closes the gate behind us he whispers that the man who wants to see me has come from the police headquarters. My heart suddenly jumps wondering what the police would want me for. But I thank BK and prepare to face the fellow boldly.

In the visitors' room, I recognise my visitor instantly. In his forties like me, it was this fellow who disposed of the African National Congress bumph, which would have implicated me in the real politics of the region when they searched our bedroom. But I don't believe he is harbinger of good news just now, and how dare he smile at me as he extends his filthy hand to offer me his handshake? I mumble something incomprehensible and immediately attack.

'Why are you people refusing to give my wife and

children visiting permits to see me? Every political prisoner here is being visited. Nobody visits me. What wrong has my family done to you?'

'The higher authorities are looking into these matters,' he answers and continues, 'Dr Mapanje, how are you?'

'How can anyone be within these stinking rotten walls? I want to go home. That's how I am! How can you help me?'

'The higher authorities are looking into that too.'

'For how long will your higher authorities go on looking into whatever it is they are looking into?'

'I don't know, anyway, Dr Mapanje, I came here because I've been sent by the higher authorities to ask you to sign this.'

'Sign what?'

'His Excellency's order for your detention.'

'What?'

'H.E.'s detention order.'

'The D.O.?'

'Yes, the D.O.'

My head reels as if from a deluge of prison guards' truncheons. I feel sick and begin sweating in the oppressive heat. A cockroach from the rafters falls on my visitor's lap; he mechanically pushes it away and watches my response. It's only last week that TS and I joked about my signing Banda's famous detention order: if it should come to signing the D.O., TS suggested, I should protest once or twice but sign it in the end. In the twelve years he has been here he had known lots of political prisoners who were abandoned by the Special Branch for refusing to sign Banda's detention order. I should not demand lawyers either because the Special Branch consider that as being confrontational to authority. I did not like the self-censorship, which TS's propositions entailed, but we were dealing with people who did not care whether one lived or died. And now this. I feel the cramps in my tummy. The bench begins to squeak. On the dirty wall of the visiting room someone crushed a mosquito that must have sucked his blood and left the bloody spot there glaring.

'But if I sign this D.O. I am accepting that I've done my country, the president or anyone in authority wrong. You know very well I have not done anyone wrong. Why do you want me to accept that I have committed a crime when you know I have not?'

'Dr Mapanje, you must ask the higher authorities these questions not me.'

'But your higher authorities refuse to show up here. You were there when the Eastern Division Commissioner of Police promised to come to see me the day you dumped me here. To date no authority has put his foot in this prison. Even Chief Commissioner of Prisons Chikanamoyo refuses to come and hear the problems I have in this prison. When do your higher authorities plan to come? And which higher authorities are you talking about, anyway?'

'Look, Dr Mapanje, I've only been sent to ask you to sign the D.O. Your signing it will solve a lot of problems. Everybody will be happy.'

'Everybody? What's this man talking about? Mister, I thought you were talking about the higher authorities a minute ago, who's this everybody you are talking about now? And why does your everybody not care about what I think, what I suffer, what my wife and children suffer, what my aging mother is suffering?'

'Look, man, I am only a messenger!'

He's right. There's no point wasting my energy quarrelling with this character; the so-called 'higher authorities' have sent this junior officer precisely for them to avoid my challenging the cockroaches! This same fellow came to see me last month on a mission he did not know I had initiated. Mercy and the children had not believed the surreptitious correspondence we had been engaged in for some time. So in a note to her I said, 'If you want to prove that I am still alive and at Mikuyu Prison, find my cheque book; take it to the Eastern Division Police Headquarters; tell them Mother, the children and you are starving; you need cash urgently; could the authorities take the blank cheques for me to sign? You can then deposit the cheques into your account and buy the food you need for the family. You'd thereby have proved I am alive and at Mikuyu Prison!' It was the perfect trick. The police fell for it and sent this man to get me to sign my cheques for Mercy. Now he brings the order for my own detention.

'Where do you want me to sign?'

'Just here, next to H.E.'s own signature, here.'

I note that Banda's signature is the usual photocopy of the original 1960 Malawi Congress Party Card, when the party fought the British for our independence. My detention order is No. 264 and the stupid piece of paper reads:

'IN EXERCISE of the powers conferred upon me by regulation 3 of the Public Security Regulations, 1965, I, H. KAMUZU BANDA, President, considering it to be necessary for the preservation of public order so to do, hereby direct that you,

JOHN ALFRED CLEMENT MAPANJE of N.A. Makanjira, V.H. Kadango, Mangochi, be detained at any place within Malawi for the time being approved by me as a prison or detention camp for the purposes of the said Regulations.

signed

H. KAMUZU BANDA PRESIDENT'

I sign my name, feel sick and disgusted, and ask BK to take me back to D4 immediately, I don't want to look at the Special Branch fellow again. I return to the cell choking with rage. Everybody knows that the meeting was disastrous; some assume I went to hear about death in the family; others think this will eventually lead to the punishment cell for somebody; before yet others begin speculating that another strip search might follow, I shout for all to hear.

'I am sorry, gentlemen, but I went to sign the D.O.,' I sigh in despair, 'It was the fellow who searched my office and my house two months ago who brought it; and I've signed it; so, please leave me alone; I want to think.' My voice begins to break.

D4 is suddenly dead. Those playing games of draughts and ludo in the courtyard or in the cell stop.

Shock and despair are written all over the cell's walls. There's a paradox. While I had not signed the detention order there was hope for me to be released. Some cellmates even believed that my being freed quickly would be good for them. I would be forced to fight for them; I had known the subhuman conditions we lived under at Mikuyu; I would therefore be the perfect ambassador for them. Others believed that my signing the detention order would mean the authorities were thinking of releasing me early. These expectations are permanently dashed now. But TS and Brown quickly come to resuscitate whatever hope is still about. We must write a note to tell the world that I've signed the dreaded D.O., which means I am here for a very long time indeed, unless someone begins shouting somewhere. We decide to tell Fr Pat, David, Landeg, our relatives, colleagues, compatriots and friends throughout the world to intensify the struggle. Yet for the rest of the day D4 refuses to leave me alone. The cellmates come one by one to offer their condolences for my signing Banda's detention order – I feel desperate, helpless and sick as if I had truly signed the warrant of my death. When I lie down brooding in bed that evening I compose a prayer, which I say regularly.

'Almighty God, too many nobler than I, have perished for the liberation of this country. Please, do not add my name to their number. Lord, do not let my torturers triumph over me, my family, relatives, friends, these innocent prisoners, those suffering in other prisons throughout the country, and those fighting for our liberation. If you will, Lord, I ask for survival not death as the major statement of protest to my torturers. And let my enemies see your light, on your own terms, not on my terms or theirs, through Jesus Christ, I pray. Amen.'

That night I have the first complete dream, which I recall in its entirety the following morning: I am strolling along a thickly wooded valley between two mountain ranges, thinking how difficult it would be to cross the river that lies in between. In a nearby cluster of reed on the riverbank I notice noses, of what can only be crocodiles, poking above the gently flowing water – anyone who crosses the river will obviously be meat for these crocodiles. But suddenly, between two branches of a nearby tree above me, I see a leopard hunched up ready to jump at anyone walking below. Before I begin to run, the beast turns at me, its jaws and paws bared and ready to attack; I instantly start to pray for God to spare my life. The beast leaps towards me, I quickly swerve to face it, ready to fight back – though goodness knows how.

All in a flash, the creature and I are fighting and struggling. The beast is trying to pin me down on the dusty ground with its paws; I am going for its jaws, the two sets of teeth should not close in on my hands, otherwise I am a dead man, I tell myself. I am struggling to press firmly at the beast's lower jaw with my right foot while both hands pull more resolutely at its upper jaw. I am pressing down hard and pulling up harder until the beast slowly begins to tear apart in two halves. The monster in me continues to desperately fight with the beast that is now kicking and writhing to its death. Eventually I notice I have, in effect, ripped the animal in half from the mouth along the ribs to its tail, its insides are out, blood is pouring all over. Breathless, sweating and covered in the beast's reeking blood, I gasp ceaselessly and feel triumphant, wondering how I'd managed to kill the fearful creature.

I wake up covered in sweat, trembling with fear, my heart still pounding fast, but delighted that I am alive. One prison guard who poked at my side with his truncheon shouts that the morning is here. Indeed the guard commanders have already opened cell D4 and the rest of the guards on their shifts are going home or taking their places in and around the prison. They have already confirmed that our number is right and we are all alive – the kind of roll-call I am trying to get used to. I stand up but find it difficult to walk. The toe on my right foot is swollen. And this is the toe that took most of the weight when my foot pressed firmly at the beast's lower jaw, as my hands tore the beast's mouth apart, in the dream – for two weeks I am unable to walk.

Estimated Time of Arrival?

Sumeia Ali

'It ain't like we've used da tickets…' Izzy trailed off. He'd suddenly gone bright red, 'We don't have any more money! What are we 'posed ta do?!'

'Sir, it is against policy to refund tickets which have been used.' The man at the help desk looked annoyed. His eyes flickered over Izzy, settling for a moment on a scar along Izzy's jawline. Nervously he turned from us, no doubt hoping we would just go away.

'What you mean against policy? They han't been used!' Izzy shouted waving the partly unused tickets under the man's nose.

'Yes, sir, they have been.'

'No…No, they han't! Only 'alf of 'em!! Are you blind? We paid for a trip ta Manchester an' a return back ta Dewsbury. We never used da return. Der woz an emergency, we had ta stay overnight. It ain't our fault!! We need ta get back…' Izzy was desperate now and I half expected him to start begging.

'I'm sorry, sir…' The man glared at Izzy, 'There's nothing I can do. The tickets are dated for use yesterday. They are therefore unusable today and as they have been partly used I cannot refund them. You must purchase two new tickets if you wish to board a train.'

'You mus' be deaf as well! A jus' said we don't 'ave any dough on us...' Izzy dropped his head into his chest and I heard him groan.

'It is possible to pay by credit card, sir.' The man glanced in my direction, his eyes begging for my intercession. I ignored his plea and watched Izzy.

'You honestly fink a would be stood 'ere, making an absolute prat of maself, if a had a credit card on me?' He glared at the man, and then suddenly seeming to remember the silent figure that stood beside him, asked, 'You don't 'appen ta have wun do ya?' to which I shook my head.

'Is there no one you can contact, sir?'

'Stop sir'in' me.' Izzy grumbled. Turning away he took my hand, 'Screw dis...' and led me towards the seats near the platforms.

'What now?' I asked playing with an arm of my jacket tied around my waist.

'Fuck me sideways, a han't a clue.' He screwed his face up, scowling, 'We dead.'

'Can't you ring Kam?'

'Ee's in hospital, innit?' Izzy looked up at the screens above our heads, 'Der's a train ta Huddersfield at 'alf past two, twenty minutes.'

'What? Do you wanna jump on?' I grinned. Further excitement was obviously coming my way. Now *this* was how I wanted to lead my life.

'You fink we should?'

'Well...It's not like we're doing anything wrong...We've paid for a return to Dewsbury. It's not our fault that it was yesterday.'

'Actually, yer it is. We shun't 'ave stayed.'

'Yeah, and if we'd have ignored Kam, he'd be dead now.'

'A know. Da guy's a dickhead though. Why da fuck does he get himself inta shit like that? Next time a ain't gonna be der.' The redness had returned to Izzy's cheeks and he frowned, curling his lip.

I turned away unimpressed, squinting against the sunlight, 'He's your brother Iz. He needed you, so you should be there.'

'No Yaz, ee needs ta grow up.'

I knew there was no arguing with Izzy when he was like this, so I chose to leave it, 'Let's sit.'

'Oh for god's sake, why you gettin' funny wit' me now?' Izzy swore under his breath and blew his hair off his forehead. He wore nothing but a t-shirt and jeans, yet he was sweating like a polar bear in a desert.

'I'm not.'

'You are. Look how you talkin' ta me…'

'I just…' I hesitated, unsure whether to challenge Izzy when he was in such a state. 'I just think you could have been easier on him at the hospital that's all.'

'WOT?!' Izzy's outburst startled several passers-by.

'The guy was nearly killed.'

Izzy spat his contempt. 'Ee shun't be so stupid.' An old woman nearby glared at him. He raised a finger and she scuttled past us muttering about cheek and manners.

I tried to calm him: 'I'm sure he won't be next time…' Izzy gaped at me, a hazy look of disbelief settling over his eyes. He chose not to answer. I don't think he trusted himself to say anything. I knew what I had said was stupid: next time (and there would definitely be a next time) would be exactly the same, maybe even worse. Izzy had been clearing up Kam's mess for as long as either of the two had been up and walking.

Izzy walked away and sat on a nearby bench. I groaned at my own stupidity and followed him over. Sitting next to him I offered an apology. He did not answer. I took his hand, he pulled away. I tried to melt the ice between us.

'I'm sorry, really.'

No answer.

'I hate when you're like this. One comment and you just go off on one.' I looked up, noticing that the old woman had returned with a much older man.

Izzy looked at me. 'Yeah, you're right…A'm jus' pissed off wit' Kam. A'm sorry, okay?'

'Yeah…So?'

'So…Jus' fuck it yeah. We'll deal wit' Kam wunce we dealt wit' our own problems. Namely how ta get home!' Izzy had now also noticed the old couple. He shot the old woman razor-tipped, poisoned daggers. The old man beside her was shaking his head.

'Well that'll be easy. Just hop on a train, hide in the loos and we're done. We can call somebody once we're in Huddersfield and we'll be home dry.'

'It ain't dat easy. We'll get caught on da train.' Izzy turned away from the old couple. I noticed his hands were shaking.

'Whoa…You're really nervous aren't you?'

He gave a shaky laugh, 'Course a am. A'm shittin' it ya know. We're so fucked! A don't believe dis is happenin'. Can't believe dey won't refund us an' a can't believe a – a can't believe we are so stupid not ta have bought extra money. Dis is not happenin'…'

'Whoa, Izzy…Stop freaking out, it'll be fine.' I took his hand in mine.

'No, it won't…A can't believe we don't have money for tickets…Dey'll catch us you know, hidin' in da bloomin' loos like bloomin' criminals, and chuck us off da train. Probably hand us inta da old bill while they're at it. Then we'll get a fine of like a grand, *den* we'll be rilly fucked.'

'I hardly doubt so.' I sat back and watched a group of children walk towards a nearby platform. They all carried lunchboxes and had identical satchels slung over their shoulders. They were laughing, excited with the journey ahead of them. I turned back to Izzy, trying to focus on the issue at hand, 'Calm down will you. Half the time they don't even check the tickets.'

'Yeah, well…Knowin' our luck dey most definitely will.' Izzy stood up and began pacing.

I slapped his leg as hard as I could, which in reality isn't that hard at all. 'Sit the fuck down, it's gonna be fine.'

'It won't be. Dey'll take wun look at me wit' ma scars an' ma clothes an' ma image, an' assume a'm up ta no good.' He ran his hands through his hair and dropped himself into the seat besides me.

'Oh shut up will you. You're gonna make me nervous. Nobody will even see us, so nobody is gonna judge you on your stupid image.' I grabbed his hand, to stop him getting up again. 'You know what? I've never realised that you are so negative about everything…'

'A know a am…A can't help it. A mean

c'mon…Look at da situation we're in! How on earth are you so calm?' He slumped further into his seat and groaned at the ceiling.

'Cos…You've got to be, innit? I'll worry about it when we're locked in the loos and the train is on the move. Until then, I might as well enjoy my freedom.' I let go of his hand and tapped his arm, 'Look they're leaving.'

He looked at the old couple. The woman obviously having lost interest had begun to walk away. The man trailed behind her, dragging a suitcase on wheels.

Izzy watched them go and then looked at me, 'You are so, amazin', actually. A wish a could be like dat. I need ta stop worrying so much.'

'Yeah, you do. So just chill out.'

'A can't…'

I laughed, 'I'm gonna have to buy you some dye for all the white hair you'll have soon.'

Izzy smiled and leant back, closing his eyes, 'Oh shut up, child.'

'Child? Is that how you talk to the love of your life? Your soul mate?'

'Yeah man, pretty much. A gotta show you oose boss.' He grinned and ran his fingers through his hair again, this time because of vanity, not nervousness.

'Yeah, whatever. You don't say that when you're cooking or cleaning.'

'A only do dat cos we ain't married. Wunce we are, it'll be your job.' He smiled to himself.

'You seriously think I'll marry you with that attitude? Just shut up yeah.' I rested my hand over his mouth, which he bit in retaliation.

'Hey…'

He smirked and, picking up a newspaper lying on the seat beside him, left me to entertain myself. The station was busy and most of the crowd dragged suitcases or had bags thrown over their shoulders. A man with green hair stood chatting to a girl with half a shaven head. Besides them stood a young Asian lad, checking his watch every couple of minutes. A young child rode on the back of an older man who made his way to a woman in a long brown coat. The woman began smothering the child in kisses, holding him close. She then placed the child on the floor and embraced the man. The little boy stood watching his parents, so tiny amongst the giants who thundered by.

'Izzy, look.' I tugged on his arm.

He looked up, 'Wot is it?'

I pointed to the little boy, 'He's so tiny…'

We sat and watched as the boy walked around his parents before attempting an escape along the tiled floor, only to be caught by his father.

'Ee's prolly only jus' started walkin' on his own you know.' Izzy smiled, one of those rare smiles which lights up his face and melts his impassive eyes, 'So cute.'

'I know…Damn, I'm not a kid person, but he is really adorable.'

Izzy nodded, 'You'll be ready for your own soon.'

'Don't make me smack you.'

He opened his mouth to argue, caught the look on my face and went back to his paper. I stood up, bored. 'You know, this is really stupid. Shall I ask someone to lend us some dosh?'

He looked at me surprised, 'Don't be daft. We ain't a coupla scrubbers, yeah.'

'You're too proud,' I tutted my disapproval.

'We ain't beggin',' he said, laying down the law.

'It's not called begging. It's called kindness and generosity.'

'Sit down, baby,' he commanded.

I looked around. It would be dumb not to try. Time to forget Izzy and his ego, 'I'm gonna go for it.'

'Don't be daft.'

'No one's asking you to come along.'

'Good. I ain't no beggar.'

'Wish me luck?'

'Sit down.'

I ignored him and began walking towards a café across from us.

'Yaz!'

I didn't turn. Waving over my shoulder, I half expected him to come after me and take me back, but he did no such thing. I entered the café and looked around. The counter stood directly beside the door, and the seating area was set at the back of the shop. There weren't many customers. I searched for a friendly looking face but got only vague stares, I decided I didn't fancy my chances. Dying for a coffee I turned to leave and saw him. He was stood in the doorway, peering in, as I had been a moment before. He was tall, very tall and reminded me of a basketball player, well built with amazing shoulders, a gorgeous tan and the sexiest legs known to man. I stood and I gaped. He was less than a metre from me and I just wanted to reach over and touch his muscular arm.

'*Ask him for money, ask him. Just talk to him, say anything,*' my mind instructed. My legs were refusing to obey instructions however so I just stood and gaped. He began walking towards me. He had the most amazing facial structure I had ever seen. He approached the counter without a second glance my way. I glared at his back and decided to leave.

'Hey! Hey, you!'

I turned. It was him.

'Wassup?' he asked. He was American. 'You okay love?' he drawled.

'Uhuh,' I nodded.

He watched me, waiting for me to speak. He was probably used to females going all coo-coo around him.

'Y-you A-american?' I stuttered, before wincing at my idiotic comment.

His laugh was amazing, deep and throaty, 'Yeah. From Cali. What about you?'

'Me? Uhh…I'm from Yorkshire. This town called Dewsbury.'

'Cool,' he said, clearly not thinking so. 'What's your name?'

'Yaz.'

'Short for?' he inquired, playing with a napkin.

'Yasmin.'

'Wow, that's nice. Tell me, why do you call yourself Yaz when you got such a nice name?'

'I dunno. Just, you know…'

'Yeah…' He nodded and beckoned to the man lazing around behind the counter, 'So you want a coffee?'

'I really should go actually.'

'Oh…Got someone waiting? Boyfriend?'

I thought of Izzy, with his newspaper. 'Not necessarily. Just, umm, I'm kinda short and I was looking around for a generous soul who'd lend me some money to get me back home.'

He laughed his deep, sexy laugh. 'You been out partying or something? Spend all your little pounds and pennies.'

I thought back to the events of last night, 'I wouldn't say party.'

'Look…' He took out his wallet and opened it. A five pound note was crumpled into a side pocket. 'I doubt that'd be enough to get you home. I'm waiting for my mate to pick me up see. Big English guy. I'd give you some if I had any.'

I smiled, touched with his honesty, 'It's cool. Don't worry about it.'

'We could wait for him. He'll be here in like an hour or so. I'm sure he'll have some on him.'

I shook my head, 'I can't. Train leaves soon.'

'Oh, I'm sorry then. Look let me get you a coffee at least, please?'

'I seriously need to go. Thanks for everything though.'

'Hold on.' He took out a pen and scribbled something onto his napkin. 'This is where I'm staying in England. I'm here for like two months so call me sometime. Or come and see me, even better. It's in Yorkshire too, place called Leeds.'

He pressed the napkin into my hand, Izzy's face flashed to mind. I opened my mouth to protest.

'What can I get you?' the man behind the counter asked. He seemed annoyed at being disturbed.

'If you're not going, I'm gonna buy you a coffee, Yaz.'

'No. Thanks. I'm going, really. Thanks again.'

He grinned, 'Hope to hear from you.'

I didn't answer. Waving, I left the café with my mouth dry and my heart thumping. For some reason I didn't throw the napkin away. It ended up scrunched up in my back pocket. No one I asked for cash was as sexy, or as nice, as him. Some simply stared, wondering if I was kidding or what. Some were apologetic, as if *they* were to blame for my lack of cash. One man told me to go get a job and stop being a scrounger and another told me to 'use my assets' and earn some money. I told him where to stick it and with my enthusiasm deflated, I returned to Izzy.

*

Yaz woz laid in ma arms. Her eyes were shut an' her hair had fallen in front of her face. She opens her eyes, dem big green stunners dat stop everywun dead in der tracks, an' looks up at me. 'You fallin' asleep on me, posh bird?' She rolls her eyes. 'Where's Jazza?' 'Gone ta sell some maal love. Ee be back soon, den we chippin' a-ight? Don't want you gettin' in shit over me at home.' A move her hair offa her face. She tells me it's a-ight an' she won't be gettin' inta no shit. A know she jus' sayin' it so a don't worry. We go quiet, watchin' da telly, when ma phone goes off. A sit up, pass her da joint, an' answer it.

'Salams bruva.' It's Kam. Kam da dick who never gets off ma fuckin' case. 'Where are you Iz?' Ee's scared a can tell. 'Wit' ma bird, b. An' before you ask, no. So fuck off.' A'd promised Yaz a'd go straight. Not jus' for her an' our future, but ta keep maself breathin'. Ee starts whinin'. Ee mus' be in some deep shit if ee's whinin' at me. 'Izzz…' *Iz dat gora called me a Paki, Izzz go break his face; Iz dem nex' boys owe me dough, Izzz make dem pay.* 'Izzz a need your help. Big time bruva. You can't jus' fuck me off.' A sit up. Yaz looks worried. A kiss her on da cheek an' leave da room. A know she hates when a freeze her out but a hate her havin' ta hear shit like dis. Especially if a'm givin' wun of ma own a bollockin'. 'Wot da fuck is da matter wit' you man?' A hope she can't hear. 'Sort yourself out, b. Dis shit gonna get you killed. Wotever it is a ain't gettin' involved.'

A push back da jaali, or as Yaz calls dem, in dat sexy posh English accent of hers, 'the net curtains'. Where da fuck is Jazza? A regret not askin' him ta drop us off at da station before ee left. 'A'll be dead if you don't.' How many times have a heard dat wun? So a tell him ta go die.

'Yeah? Den wot you gonna tell Mom? *Amee, amee, a couldn't be arsed goin' ta help out Kam. Now ee's dead. But it's a-ight. 'Cuz ee a waster anyway.*' A tense up. 'Don't you dare bring ma mother inta dis, b.' A'd told her about Yaz da other night. A'd told her a loved her an' wanted ta marry da girl. A'd expected her ta go berserk but she never. She'd said dat if a did it'd be da biggest mistake of ma life. 'Ismaeil bayta, kuriya over here. They no good. One day they will leave you. Get married to

88

good Pakistani kuri from back home. Aunty Semina has a daughter. Your age. Very good cook. Tell me, can this kuri cook?' When a'd told her no, she'd shook her head. 'See bayta. No good. You will starve.' A'd told her dat Yaz would learn. 'No bayta. All kuriya from here want career. Big career.' A would have actually preferred a beatin'…Yaz had gone mad when a told her a'd told ma mom. She goes dat a rilly should have asked her firs'. A knew she woz right but it were a little late ta go back. At least now Yaz knows dat a'm well serious about me an' her.

Kam whines, 'A'm her son anall. We blood, or you forgot? If she cries over me, dat's on your head bruva.' A shake ma head an' tell him 'No b, it's on yours. You got yourself inta dis shit, a din't make you.' Den ee's feedin' me da same old promises dat a hear every time: 'A swear Iz. Never again. Dis be serious though. Hanson comin' down.' Ma heart goes all funny, like flu'ery, like when a see Yaz for da firs' time on a day. Only it's not a happy flu'ery, it's a scared adrenaline filled, fearful flu'ery. 'Fuck dat. You got beef with Hanson? Wot you done ta piss him off?' You don't mess with Hanson. Hanson knows ee's goin ta hell an' ee ain't scared. Hanson's wun crazy mofo.

Kam goes quiet. Dat means it mus' be rilly stupid if ee ain't man enough ta tell me. 'You khota, wot is it?' Ee don't answer. Den quietly ee goes, 'A'm sorry.' Ee's shittin' himself, a can tell. An' as usual ee's callin' me ta sort his shit out. 'Wot you done Kam? Tell me now or else I'm hangin' up an' ma phone's turnin' off.' But Kam's no man. Fuckin' batty boy, no blood a mine. Ee's stutterin' 'A-a-a…'

So a hang up. An' go back ta Yaz. She doesn't question. Thank fuck. But her eyes are demandin' an explanation. 'Kam's in shit. Again.' A take da joint back off her. It's out so a light it back up. 'You not smokin' babes?' She wrinkles her nose an' shakes her head. 'Is he going to be alright, Iz?' 'Ee will be, gorguz.' Her eyes are scannin' me. Ma phone starts up again. She watches as a turn it off. 'What's the matter?' If I say nutin' I know she won't leave it, but if I mention Hanson she's gonna make me go help. Cuz she knows all 'bout Hanson an' wot ee does ta peeps ee got any typa beef wit'. A'd told her wunce 'bout how Hanson had shot a man, all 'cuz ee had some beef with him over some cars dat needed shiftin'. Supposedly dis dude had been rippin' Hanson off. Hanson hadn't waited for da facts. Ee hadn't even gone over an' gave him wot's wot. Jus' shot him an' left. Der woz a strong chance dat da dude was innocent but no wun's gonna dare mention dat. Fuck no, unless dey suicidal or some shit.

She din't let it go though. An' by da time Jazza's back a've told her all a know. A know we ain't gettin' home tonight. Fuckin' Kam an' his fucktard idiocy. She tells me 'Make sure he's okay, baby. C'mon…' An' 'cuz she's so worried a listen an' we leave a minute or so later. Only 'cuz a love her. Dis got nowt ta do wit dat kameena who calls himself ma bro.

*

'What time's the train?'

Izzy glanced up smiling, 'Well?'

I shook my head. 'No luck. Don't you start with *I told you so.*'

'Promise a won't.' He looked up at a digital clock which hung over the customer service desk, 'Train's now, actually.' He turned in his chair and pointed through the glass windows at the platform behind us, 'Dat'll be ours.'

'We definitely doing this then?' I asked, swallowing hard. Now that crunch time had arrived, I could feel myself beginning to panic.

'We don't have much ov a choice.' He got up, stretched and offered me a hand which I took. We made our way to the train and before we boarded he looked at me, 'Second stop Yaz, second stop is Huddersfield.'

I nodded, suddenly silent. Izzy smiled, 'A guess dis is da point where you get nervous too.'

I nodded again, unsure whether to brave words. He led me onto the train and, hand-in-hand, we made our way to the end carriage. We sat opposite each other outside the loos. The reality of the situation now having dawned upon me, I closed my eyes and muttered a quiet prayer.

The train began filling up. There weren't many seats going spare.

'Are we gonna go in now, or at the first stop Iz?' I chewed my thumb nail.

'Firs' stop. Dey never check before den anyway.'

The train shuddered into life and the sudden rattling of the floor and walls dominated my thoughts. Izzy watched the doors: our final route of escape. Then slowly they began to close and a look of helplessness passed over his face. We were now trapped with no hope of deserting our mad plan.

He smiled weakly, 'Dat's us done for.'

I didn't answer. I was now more than just a little nervous myself. The train began to pull away. A woman's voice rang out through the intercom announcing each and every stop the train would be making and that passengers should get their tickets ready for inspection as she was about to make her way through the train.

I began laughing. Izzy stared.

'Wot's so funny? Dis is bad news…'

'Nothing's funny. Leave me alone.'

Izzy rolled his eyes. I stood and went over to the nearest loo only to find it blocked with wads of toilet roll.

'Not this one,' I said holding my nose.

'Stop bein' so picky Yaz, we don't have much ov a choice.' Izzy tried the loo opposite. I heard the toilet flush and then he reappeared, 'Get in before a lock you out.'

'You would never…'

He smiled a sickly sweet smile which I did not feel like challenging. Together we squeezed into the toilet and locked the door behind us. I set down the lid of the loo, feeling a little sick. We stood in silence as the train rattled along. A couple of times somebody walked by and we both stiffened in panic. A little while later the train pulled into its first stop and we both breathed a sigh of relief.

'Wun down,' Izzy mouthed causing me to giggle. He put a finger to my lips, signalling silence, and I mouthed an apology. He smiled and put his arms around me as passengers walked by outside our door. I wrapped my arms around his solid torso, feeling partly safe.

'You know what?' I whispered into his chest.

'Yeah?'

'When we're both at home tonight, we're gonna laugh about this and wonder why we were so scared.' I smiled.

He chuckled quietly. The train started up again a couple of minutes later and his grip around my body loosened.

'How long until we get to our stop?' I asked.

Izzy's eyes darted quickly from the door to me, 'Shh…Don't talk so loud…'

I whispered, 'No one's gonna hear us over the noise of the engine.'

Izzy leaned his mouth near my ear, 'A don't wanna take *any* chances.'

I rolled my eyes at his extreme paranoia and tapped his watch, 'How long?'

'A dunno…'Bout 'alf an hour, twenty minutes ma–' He cut himself short and his eyes bulged in his head, his hand gripping my arm.

'Wha–' I began, Izzy jammed a hand over my mouth. With his other hand he pointed at the door handle. I looked down. The door handle was moving: someone was trying to get in.

*

Hanson's dead eyes are starin' at me. 'Bruva, enough respect, but sometimes somethin's over step da mark by way too much.' Kam's sprawled on da pavement. Blood seepin' down his face. His left leg's atta weird angle an' ee's whimperin' as ee stares up at me. 'A know wot you mean, but dis ma bro we chattin' about.' Two of Hanson's boys stand at either side of him. Kam's crew have been silenced. Dey stand huddled together, scared as fuck. Dey know wot's comin' if a don't sort dis shit out.

Hanson's smirkin' at me. Mockin' me. 'You ain't even from these parts no more bruva. You got no power no more. Your don days are over.' A look away tired of all these pathetic games. Who da fuck cares how much fuckin' dope you shift or how many wankers you got runnin' your errands? 'True b, true. But for old times sake a'm askin' ya.' Ee laughs an' his boys join in. 'Don't you ever get tired of coverin' his arse man? If a were you a'd have done da deed maself by now.'

A glance back at Jazza's car. A can't see Yaz through da blacked out windows but know she's der. 'Listen. A'll tie you over wit' wotever ee owes you okay? Jus' name da price an' a'll get it ta you. Den a promise ee'll never be in your face again.' Suddenly everythin's so much more serious. 'Ain't as simple as dat bruva. You fink a'd come down maself ta tie over a simple debt?' A sigh. Of course not. Kam never does thin's simply. 'So wot is it den?' Der's silence. 'WOT IS IT?' A know it's not a good thin' to be shoutin'. You don't shout at Hanson. Unless you're stupid. Ee laughs again. Dat dry laugh. 'So wot, ee never had da balls ta tell you himself?' Of course not. Kam's got no fucking balls. 'Wot's ee done?' A close ma eyes. A'm not sure a actually wanna know. Den comes da answer: 'Ee has da balls ta send his boys dealin' down our ends. My ends. Not only dat. Ma bird.' Ma heart stops. 'Of all of dem out der, ee comes for mine.'

A feel like goin' over an' stickin' wun on Kam maself. A have nutin' ta say. A'm shocked inta stupidity an' a'm left gapin'. A glance back. Yaz's not safe der. She should be home in front of da fire in dem grubby old slippers of hers. Kam's eyes are closed, ee's prayin', prayin' for his life. I tell Hanson, 'Wotever you want bro. Anythin'. Jus' tell me an' you got it.' 'Wot's a man like you got ta possibly offer a man like me? You're a loser bro. You gave up all dis.' Ee gestures round, 'All your power, everythin' for some hoe.' A spit at him. 'Wot like your bird's turned out ta be? You may have everythin', but a got her an' dat's all a need.' Not a good idea ta be attackin' him. 'You ain't helpin' matters bro. You meant ta be diggin' your family outta shit not heapin' more on yourselves.'

A'm silent. Said enough stupid thin's for tonight. Then ee sez, 'Wot's her name?' Ma breath cuts short in ma throat. 'Why?' Ee steps forward. 'A wanna know da name of da bitch who melted da hardest thug a ever knew.' 'Yaz.' A'm whisperin' now. A don't want dis shit affectin' her. She got nowt ta do wit' it. 'Tell me Iz. If it came down ta it, who would you pick: him, your blood, or her?' Der's no hesitation. 'Her.' Kam's opened his eyes, ee's starin' at me again. Hanson smiles coldly. 'Her. A want her.' A back up. Ma heart's bangin'. 'You said it yourself. A have everythin'. Da only thin' you have ta offer me is her.' Fuck Kam. Fuck it all. Dis is his shit. Yaz ain't gettin' involved. A'm whisperin' again as a carry on backin' up. Da car's only a few yards away. Hanson can see ma fear. Ee knows ee's struck a soft spot. 'You give me her an' a'll let you walk away.' A shake ma head. 'She ain't got nowt ta do wit' it. You an' Kam. You two sort it out. A've done ma bid, put in ma good word. A'm out.'

Ee signals ta wun of his thugs who goes over an' drags out wun of Kam's sissy boys. Ee's nutin' but a kid. Wot, seventeen? Eighteen? 'It's too late bruva. You're involved. Dis your business now.' Da lad's shiverin'. Ee's pissin' himself. A shake ma head. 'You'd rather lose your bruva's life, all these boys' lives, as well as your own, over some bitch?' A stare him in da eyes. If a'm gonna die a might as well die like a man. 'A'd lose anythin' for her.' Hanson points ta da car. 'Go fetch. A know she's der. A seen her when you got outta car.' A shake ma head again. Hanson's thug squeezes da young lad. Hansons growls: 'Don't make me ask you twice.'

*

I looked up at Izzy, his face was void of all expression. My mind screamed '*Go away, go away!!*' at the person on the other side of the door. Telepathy must have occurred because they obeyed, a moment later the handle stopped moving. I felt the colour surge back into my face as I listened to them walk away. Izzy let out a long sigh and sat down on the toilet. He dragged a finger across his throat making me laugh.

The ticket lady must not have 'check the loos' on her agenda because the remainder of the journey was pretty eventless. Several times we were disturbed by people wanting the loo. I wondered why people couldn't read that the toilet was 'occupied'.

As the train rattled into Huddersfield station we unlocked the door and scuttled out. The aisle was crowded with people, some stared as we came out together. Izzy bowed his head, his face red. I felt a giggle rising from the pits of my belly, which I swallowed, causing me to hiccup. Forcing myself to be serious, I stared at my feet and avoided eye contact.

As the doors opened we followed the crowd onto the platform and jogged towards the exit. Once safe on the steps outside, Izzy collapsed into hysterics.

'I can't believe we've made it.' I said, half expecting someone to come running out after us to make us pay for our crime.

'A know…Wow, you shoulda seen your face back den…' He laughed.

'Dude, you should have seen yours,' I sat down on the stairs. 'God I'm tired. My feet are hurting like fuck from standing for so long.'

He sat down and put his arm around me, 'At least you ain't bored when you wit' me.'

'You can say that again…' I rested my head on his shoulder and closed my eyes, 'Right, now to get back to Dewsbury.'

'We'll prolly end up having to walk ya know.'

'Yup, knowin' our luck…'

We sat in silence. A row of taxis were parked to the right of us and a number of taxi drivers were stood gathered together. A young Chinese woman was taking pictures of the station behind us. I ran my fingers through my hair, aware I looked wired.

'Izzy?'

'Yeah baby?'

'You know...Last night.'

Izzy rose to his feet, turning away. 'Wot have a said about talking about that world, Yaz?'

'I know I jus–'

'No Yaz. I don't want you affected by dat shit.'

A group of pigeons, startled by a young child, fluttered away to perch on a building opposite us. Izzy was silent.

'You can't bottle it all away Izzy. I want you to be able to talk about these things with me. We've avoided last night all day.'

'Wot would you have preferred a do? Hand you over ta some mad man?' He takes out a pack of cigarettes and lights one. Sitting back down, he passes me the packet. 'It will be fine.' His voice didn't seem very convincing and his hand shook as he raised the cigarette for another drag.

'But it won't Izzy. You know that.'

'Stop it Yaz! What am a supposed ta do?'

'All I'm saying is that it won't go away.'

'Look. Ee got wot he deserved. All of his boys did. There were no other way out.'

I dropped my head into my hands, 'This is all my fault. I made you go.'

'No. It's Kam's fault. Don't beat yourself up.' He put his arms around me and kissed the top of my head.

'Will they come after us?'

'Me...'

'Us, baby. *Us.*'

*

Yaz returns ta da scene wit' me. Around fifteen pairs of eyes watch her walk by my side. Da bitch who melted da heart of da hardest thug dey'd ever known. But it's all envy. Cuz dey know dey could never be so happy.

'So dis is her?' A nod, silent. It won't be long now. Jazza's already got the engine running, waitin' ta leave. Yaz is as calm as fuck. Can't believe a single person can have so much faith in me.

'Wow. A can see why you love her so much.' A don't bother arguin'. Yaz knows why am wit' her. Hanson can go screw himself. A feel like punchin' him in the mouth for oglin' at her. But der's hardly any point. Ee gonna be gone soon.

Ee starts goin' on 'bout da past. How it was thanks ta mine an' his friendship dat da blacks and Pakis had 'undestandin's'. A'd hardly view it as a friendship, but a let him go on. The longer ee talks, the more chance we got.

An' soon we can hear dem. In da distance. A sound which a had wunce feared an' ran from. A swallow hard. Dis is wun thin' no wun can ever go back on. Dey would be condemned for da rest of der lives. But it's worth it. Cuz it's for Yaz. Hanson's still talkin'. Ee tells me that a am where a am today cuz of him. An' if a han't known him no wun would have, an' a would have been nutin'. Would have been just another wannabie lookin' for a quick way outta dis hell. Der gettin' closer. You can't miss the noise now. But ee don't stop talkin'. Why should ee? Da sirens mean nutin' ta him. A mean, who would grass up the most notorious gangster around? But like dey say, love makes fools of even kings.

The Authors

'Gone to the Dogs (Madame)' by Alecia McKenzie is published in *Stories From The Yard* published by Peepal Tree Press, Leeds.   www.peepaltreepress.com

The poem 'Scrubbing the Furious Walls of Mikuyu' is from *The Last Of The Sweet Bananas, New And Selected Poems* by Jack Mapanje, published by Bloodaxe Books.

Alecia McKenzie was born and raised in Kingston, Jamaica, has worked in the USA and Belgium, and now lives in Singapore. Her first collection of stories won the Commonwealth Writers Prize for Best First Book, her latest collection is published by Peepal Tree in Leeds. **MY Alam's** two novels are set in the inner city of his home, Bradford, and are published by Route www.route-online.com. **Jack Mapanje's** career as one of Southern Africa's leading poets and academics in linguistics, was interrupted by a period of political imprisonment in Malawi, he now lives in York and is working on his prison diaries. **Sumeia Ali** was born in Bristol but moved to Yorkshire a year later and now lives in Dewsbury. This is her first published story.

For more biography and background on all the Light Transports writers go to **www.light-transports.net**

Ideas Above Our Station

ISBN 1 901927 28 8
Price £8.99

Someone is waiting for a train, or it could be a bus or an aeroplane. They are alone. For company, in their coat pocket they are carrying a book of stories. They sit down and take out the book. It falls open on the first page of a new story. What would be the perfect read for them to find there?

Fifteen writers have risen to the challenge to put the ideal story into their fellow traveller's hand. The results are inside this book.

Ideas Above Our Station is a title in the acclaimed Route series of contemporary stories.

'Sharp, refreshing and full of surprises…a bit like going to a party and meeting one fascinating person after another.'

'Route is a trailblazing publisher of literary talent. Here you'll find some of the best short storytelling since Raymond Carver.'

For details of this book and our full books programme, including the new downloadable byteback books, please visit

www.route-online.com

Route's Byteback Books

Dog Days
Editor: Katherine Locke

Dog Days: the ancient Romans noticed that the hottest days of the year, in late July and early August, coincided with the Dog Star - aka Sirius, aka The Great Dog - being in the same part of the sky as the Sun.

This powerful collection of stories is scorched with summer heat, it features people and dogs and the first flowering of love. An emotional and hazy landscape, *Dog Days* will put a sun tan on your soul.

Brief Lives
Editor: Susan Tranter

Four seasons in one day. A world in a grain of sand. A life in one story.

How can short stories ever give us more than a passing glimpse into other people's lives? What exactly *is* a life story, and how can it be told in so few words? Can short fiction deal with anything more than fragments of time?

Here are four stories from four writers which explore some very different lives. In the process, they reveal the capacity of the short story to convey much more than snapshots of time. Each offers an engaging perspective on the telling of individual and linked life stories.

Happy Families
Editor: Oliver Mantell

Four stories about families by four distinctive and

compelling storytellers: the love, the lies, the laughter, the loss. Happy Families features stories by Alexandra Fox, Penny Feeny, Chrissie Ward and Sean Burn.

Bloom

Editor: Emily Penn

Short and very short fiction exploring the realities of life in twenty first century Britain by the flower of our youth. Seven writers aged nineteen to thirty describe the now and the near future in this witty, enigmatic and engaging selection of stories.

Taking in the experience of first love, first jobs, urban desolation and a journey into the dark heart of rural Britain, this collection showcases a host of new writing talent well worth discovering.

Bitter Sky

Zdravka Evtimova

A sequence of short stories following the fortunes of Mona, the precious only daughter of Rayo the Blood. This is a warm and highly rewarding piece of storytelling from one of Bulgaria's leading writers. Bitter Sky reveals the nature of power and vanity in all its complexity and plays witness to the transformation of Bulgaria from a former part of the Eastern Block to part of the emerging new Europe.

Think hardback, paperback and now, byteback.
E-books that are also real books.
A full list of byteback titles and instructions on
how to make them up can be found at:
www.route-online.com

Other Route Books

Route Compendium
ISBN 1 901927 24 5
Price £8.99
Route Compendium is a festival of contemporary stories that brings together five of the first wave of Route's pioneering byteback books. Inside you will find five distinctive and original collections of contemporary fiction featuring: a showcase of bright young talent; the decorator's tale; stories of love and the trouble it can bring; modern folk tales and a collection of misfits which includes the most audacious car chase short story that you will probably ever read.

Wonderwall
ISBN 1 901927 24 5
Price £8.99
The Wonderwall is a spy hole into the world of other people. Meet Bradley, with his pointy shoes and his cloak; witness what transpires with Vernon, the pools-win baby; find out which coffee-shop serves the best scrambled eggs in Antarctica; see George measure his life in terms of how many biscuits he might eat; travel to the beach of the cocco-bella man.

A baker's dozen of wondrous stories that point a finger to the magic that exists within our day-to-day lives, and to the people who matter most, those close at hand.

Naked City

ISBN 1 901927 23 7

Price £8.95

At the heart of the modern city we find stories of lovers, stories of people with a desire to connect to someone else, something else. This collection reveals the experience of living through changing times, of people shaking the past and dreaming of better days, people finding their place, adapting to new surroundings, laughing and forgetting, living and loving in the grip of the city.

Included are a series of naked city portraits as seen through the lens of photographer Kevin Reynolds and a selection of the very best in new short fiction in a bonus section, *This Could Be Anywhere*.

Jack and Sal

Anthony Cropper

ISBN 1 901927 21 0

Price £8.95

Jack and Sal, two people drifting in and out of love. Jack searches for clues, for a pattern, for an explanation to life's events. Perhaps the answer is in evolution, in dopamine, in chaos theory, or maybe it can be found in the minutiae of domesticity where the majority of life's dramas unfold. Here, Anthony Cropper has produced a delicately detailed account of a troubled relationship, with a series of micro-stories and incidents that recount the intimate lies, loves and lives of Jack and Sal and their close friend Paula.

Kilo
M Y Alam
ISBN 1 901927 09 1
Price £6.95
Khalil Khan had a certain past and an equally certain future awaited until gangsters decided to turn his world upside down. They shattered his safe family life with baseball bats but that's just the beginning. They turned good, innocent and honest Khalil into someone else: Kilo, a much more unforgiving and determined piece of work. Kilo cuts his way through the underworld of Bradford street crime, but the closer he gets to the top of that game, the stronger the pull of his original values become.

Psychicbread
Mark Gwynne Jones
ISBN 1 901927 20 2
Price £6.95
Psychicbread introduces Mark Gwynne Jones and the space between our thoughts. Drawing on an ancient tradition, these captivating, mind altering poems tackle the complexities of our changing world with a beautiful humour. This collection presents the word in print, audio and film, coming complete with a CD of poems and stories.

Four Fathers

Ray French, James Nash, Tom Palmer, John Siddique

ISBN 1901927 27 X

Price £8.99

Here, four sons reveal the complex bonds that exist between themselves and their very different fathers; they then turn the tables and consider their own roles as fathers and father figures. These tender and heart warming tales mix fact with fiction and provide a perfect backdrop to reflect on this most important relationship.

Howl for Now

A celebration of Allen Ginsberg's epic protest poem

ISBN 1 901927 25 3

Price £9.99

In *Howl for Now*, academics, commentators and practitioners reflect on the power of 'Howl', half a century on from Ginsberg's historic first reading, through a series of essays and interviews.

Poet David Meltzer reflects on the San Francisco scene in the mid-1950s, Ginsberg collaborator Steven Taylor offers a personal memoir, film director Ronald Nameth and rock composer Bill Nelson contemplate a documentary version of 'Howl', and members of the University of Leeds consider the political, cultural and aesthetic place of the poem as both a social document and a point of contemporary inspiration.

Light Transports

Light Transports is a series of three books, distributed free at train stations across Yorkshire in October 2006 as part of the Illuminate Festival. Each book is filled with stories appropriate for different journey lengths; *A Couple Of Stops*, *Commutes* and *Intercity*.

A Couple Of Stops
ISBN 1 901927 29 6
Featuring stories from Winifred Holtby, Tom Spanbauer, Mandy Sutter, Steven Hall, Ellen Osborne, Chenjerai Hove and Kath McKay.

Commutes
ISBN 1901927 30 X
Featuring stories from Alecia McKenzie, MY Alam, Jack Mapanje and Sumeia Ali.

Intercity
ISBN 1901927 31 8
Featuring stories from Storm Jameson, Mark McWatt, Patricia Duncker and Aritha van Herk.

For more details visit www.light-transports.net

**For more books from Route
visit www.route-online.com**